COUNTY LINES

PHIL HOLMES

County Lines

Copyright © 2025 to Phil Holmes

www.philsholmes.com

This book is a work of fiction. Names, characters, places and
incidents either are products of the author's imagination or are
used fictitiously. Any resemblance to actual persons, living or
dead, events, or locales is entirely coincidental.

Cover design and formatting by www.letsgetbooked.com

1

Wednesday

"I told you, I've had enough," cried the young lad into his telephone as he leant his bicycle against a high, brick garden wall on a quiet street on the edge of Harrogate town. "I wanna go home."

"Listen to me, boy," shouted the man at the other end. "I'm losing patience with you. This is the third time in a week we've had this conversation. We can't let you go; you know too much. You're in this for the long haul now, so stop fucking around and tell me you're one of us."

The boy leant back against the wall and pulled the hoodie farther down over his face to hide the bruises from his last encounter with his handler, as well as the tears streaming down his face. He was only thirteen years old; he just wanted to go home.

"You think I wanna see you again?" he blurted. "After the fucking beating you gave me? No way!"

"Listen, boy, I explained that. It's about respect, innit. You were getting cocky and stupid in front of other lads. I had to set an example, yeah? You need to use your loaf, play the game, do what I tell you, and you'll have everything you ever wanted."

"I just wanna go home, see my mum."

"Bullshit!" yelled the handler. "That's all gone now, it's over. You understand me? It's history. You're one of us now, kiddo. And you're on the brink of making real money, yeah? You don't need no family, bro. No school or none of that bollocks. You just do what I tell you and I'll see you get all the money you ever dreamed of. And girls too, does that sound good? You ever been with a girl before? Tell you what, you get on your bike, take that cocaine to the punter, and I'll see you get laid as soon as you're back in the trap house. That sound like a plan?"

The young lad was silent as he contemplated the mess he was in. He had been missing for over two months, having been groomed and forced into travelling far away from home to deliver drugs to clients in and around the town of Harrogate in North Yorkshire. At first, he didn't care about what his mother must have been going through, worrying about her only son, wondering if he was alive or dead, and if alive where he was. But after being forced into taking part in activities he wanted nothing to do with, all the while being beaten and abused, all he wanted now was the safety and security of his mum.

As he prepared himself to shout into the phone, to tell the monster on the other end in no uncertain terms that he was never going back, he heard a sound. A voice over the phone, but not the handler; it was someone at the other end whispering to the handler. He heard words but was unable to make sense of most of them. He thought he may have heard "I see him", followed shortly after by "thirty seconds".

"What's that?" said the kid.

"Nothing for you to worry about, sunshine. So, listen to me, kiddo, are you delivering that fucking marching powder or not?"

"Not!" shouted the lad at the top of his voice. "You can fuck off! I'm going home. Just fuck off!"

He terminated the call, shut the phone down and threw it over the wall behind him into a garden, grabbed his bike and pedalled away. He wanted to head for the train station, get a train to Leeds then make his way back over the Pennines and home. He wanted to see his mum. There would be awkward questions to answer of course, but he liked the thought of eating some good food and sleeping in his own bed that night.

He'd made it to the end of the road and turned the corner towards the town centre when a figure appeared in front of him, forcing him to stop abruptly. An older boy stood in his way, maybe about seventeen or eighteen years old, a familiar face. He knew him from somewhere. He had an odd look about him, and appeared to be shaking a little as if he was scared of something. But there was no time to stop and chat. He needed to get away, and fast.

"Sorry, mate," he said as he went to pass him.

"Not so fast," said the teenager. "I've got something here for you."

As he tried to pass by and head towards the station, he saw something in the youth's hand that glistened in the streetlight. It was a blade, but before he could react, the young man's arm swung out, the knife heading towards his groin, hitting him at the top of his right leg. It was a wild, aimless thrust, but the blade penetrated into his flesh, causing a sudden burst of intense pain.

It happened so fast, and was so unexpected, that he was too slow to react and prevent a second strike. The knife had been withdrawn from his groin and thrust towards him again, this time striking him below his chest, piercing his clothing and cutting deep into his abdomen.

The teenager withdrew the knife and stabbed him once again, this time in the stomach, twisting the blade before withdrawing it and dropping it into a bag.

"The boss sends his fondest regards," stammered the attacker before turning away and running back down the road.

The boy, still on his bicycle, had instinctively covered his wounds with his hands. He looked down and was alarmed to see blood soaking his clothing and spurting out of his groin. Now he understood those whispered words; they had tracked him. His evil handler had sent someone to take care of his little problem. An assassin. An assassin he had seen before and knew. It was Jamie.

The boy didn't feel any real pain as he would have expected, just a numb feeling. His hands could feel the warmth of the blood, his nostrils scented the strong metallic odour. He needed help, urgently. An ambulance would be the obvious option, but as he thought about it, he knew that would mean the police would be involved. Then again, that would be better than dying. He began to feel weak. He had to make that call and started to reach for his phone but remembered he had thrown it away. Should he go back and look for it? He couldn't remember how far back it was to where he'd left it. He would have to ask for help, but there was no one around. He needed to shout.

"Hel…" he squeaked. He couldn't get the word out, and he was getting even weaker. He was tired and cold all of a sudden and felt an urge to sit down. He managed to dismount and kick his bike away before leaning back against a high metal garden fence where he stood, arms wrapped around his torso for a few seconds before slowly sliding down and sitting on the pavement. Everything was getting darker.

He tried to look around, up and down the street, hoping to see someone. Lights were on in most of the houses, but no one was out on the street. He was alone.

The young boy was losing energy and eased himself down onto his side. He knew he should get up and make his way to the nearest front door and knock until someone came to help, but he couldn't. He was helpless.

He looked down once again at his wounds, shocked at the amount of blood on the pavement. He was dying. Was that movement nearby? Maybe someone was coming. Unable to focus on whatever was heading towards him, he assumed it was the attacker returning to finish him off, and with no strength remaining, he accepted his fate. As the lights faded, his eyes closed and darkness enveloped him.

2

Detective Chief Inspector Rosie Marks had been making her way home after a busy day at the station, when she received word of an incident on the edge of town. When her colleague Detective Sergeant Fazli Masoud told her it was a stabbing, and that the reports indicated that it looked like the victim was one of the lads they had started to target and watch, she immediately diverted and made her way to the scene.

Rosie's fingers brushed her straight shoulder-length brunette hair back over her right ear as she stood by the roadside looking down at the young man. She had arrived at the scene within ten minutes of the assault, but not as quickly as other officers and, more importantly an ambulance which had been called by a neighbour who had seen the boy collapsing as she returned home from work. The timing was good, as another few minutes would have been too late.

Even now, there was little chance for the young lad. The medics were fighting to save his life, trying to relocate the faint pulse they had detected when they arrived while discussing how they would lift him up to the ambulance so they could get him to hospital as quickly as possible. It wasn't looking good for him.

Rosie's eyes drifted over to the bicycle, lying flat on the bloodstained pavement, and shook her head. He had lost a lot of blood, but the medics weren't giving up, which was good to see. This was someone's son, someone's friend, maybe someone's brother.

Rosie had been heading home to spend some quality time with the love of her life, her young daughter Sophie, when the call from Faz came through. She had called her mother to explain the delay before going to check out the incident.

The nationwide problem of county lines had spread its evil web over most of the country, and Harrogate was no exception. An OCG boss from a large city would place dealers in towns and rural areas, using a dedicated mobile phone number that potential customers could use to order illicit drugs. Local runners, often young teenage boys, many of whom were on bikes for speed and efficiency, were then sent to make those deliveries. The runners often worked under duress and extreme force, and the price for noncompliance or failure of any kind could be brutal.

Many youngsters and other vulnerable members of society were being targeted by county lines gangs, and Rosie, who headed up Operation Caterpillar, a local team fighting county lines, was determined to stamp out its evil effects on her patch.

Rosie wondered if the young lad she was looking at had been such a victim. She thought she had seen him around recently, or perhaps his photo was pinned to the board back at the incident room, but it was hard to tell in the dark and with paramedics in her line of sight. As she tried to get

11

a better look at the lad's face, she was shocked out of her thoughts by a shout.

"I've got a pulse!" said one of the medics. "He's alive."

"Oh my god," shouted the other. "Come on, he's a fighter this one. Let's help him."

Rosie watched as the reinvigorated medical team found extra enthusiasm and energy to keep the young lad alive. As they worked, something caught her eye about fifty metres away on a street corner. A small crowd had gathered to see what was going on, only being kept at a safe distance by uniformed coppers. What Rosie had seen were two young lads on bikes peering around members of the public to see what was happening. Rosie turned slowly and walked away from the scene towards a nearby police officer.

"It's Charlie, isn't it?" she said to the officer.

"Yes, boss. How can I help you?"

"Don't make it obvious by looking now, but to my left are a couple of lads on bikes. Can you organise a few officers to get close and apprehend them before they vanish? I'd like a word with them."

"Leave it with me."

"Thank you, Charlie."

Rosie turned and saw the medics carefully lift the injured boy onto a stretcher and into the ambulance. Within seconds the sirens wailed, the blue lights flashed, and the emergency vehicle was on its way to the local Harrogate hospital.

Well, well, thought Rosie. Never, ever give up. The poor boy is alive, albeit only just, and still has a chance.

12

Her thoughts were once again disturbed by a commotion. She looked over and saw four officers around the two young lads on bikes. Rosie walked over.

"Thanks, guys, and well done, Charlie," said Rosie before looking at the young lads. The last thing they wanted was to talk to the police, but they'd been caught unawares. Before they could react, PC Charlie Mills and three colleagues had them penned in and trapped. "So, what would you two be up to?"

"Nothing, miss," blurted one of them, his face partially covered by his baseball cap, which in turn was covered by his hoodie. "Honest."

"Honest, eh?" said Rosie smiling. "I wonder how honest you really are. Tell me, who is that young lad on his way to hospital?"

"Dunno," they replied in unison.

"Then how come I've seen you both in town with him recently?"

Rosie was lying, looking for a reaction, testing, probing, hoping for something useful. One of the lads spoke again.

"We hang out together sometimes, that's all."

"So you do know him then," said Rosie as she leant down a little, trying to get a better look at the boys' faces. One looked familiar.

"Not really," said the other kid.

"What's his name?"

"Who?"

"The young lad in the ambulance of course. The one you hang out with."

"Oh, it's Louie."

13

"Does Louie have a surname?" Rosie continued, still racking her brain trying to remember how she recognised one of them. They were both trying to keep their faces away from the light, caps and hoodies pulled down as far as they would go.

"Don't know. We just know him as Louie."

"Okay, so what exactly do you do with Louie when you hang out with him?"

"Nothing. Just hang out in town."

"Okay, but doing what exactly?" asked Rosie, getting a little exasperated.

"Just hanging. Getting Maccy D's, looking for girls, having a laugh."

"How about dealing drugs?" Rosie was trying to look into their eyes, testing their reactions to such a direct question. They both kept avoiding eye contact while instinctively raising their hands to cover their mouths, a common sign of lying.

"We ain't dealing drugs," stuttered one.

"No way," added the other.

"In that case," said Rosie, "you won't mind if we take a look in your pockets, will you?"

"Have you got a search warrant?"

"I might need a search warrant when I come to your home, lad," said Rosie. "But I won't need one while we're out on the street. And in any case, as you're not dealing drugs, you're going to show me what's in all your pockets, right?"

The two boys looked at each other and shrugged shoulders. One started to empty his pockets, the other followed. They both had sweets, one had a pack of tissues, neither had a phone, nor were they carrying anything illegal, certainly not drugs. Just the usual things normal teenage boys would be carrying, except a phone which Rosie found odd in this day and age. She suspected they had been sent to check out the scene by someone, a handler perhaps, who had made sure they were clean. If so, Rosie knew they would be reporting the fact that the knife victim was alive.

"Okay, lads," she said. "So, what are you going to tell your boss?"

"What?" asked one of the boys.

"When you get back, you know, and get your phones back, what are you going to tell your boss about what you've seen here?"

"Er, nothing."

"Nothing? Really? Why don't I believe you?"

"I dunno."

"Well," Rosie continued, looking right into their eyes again. "Will your boss be pleased or angry when you tell him that lad was still alive?"

There was no answer from them. Rosie was losing patience, but didn't want to let them go yet, not until she could remember where she'd seen one of them before. Suddenly it came to her.

"Oh my god," she said, looking at the boy in question. "I've got it. It's George, isn't it? George Potter, of course. I knew you looked familiar."

The boy finally looked up at Rosie. It was definitely him, son of her friend and colleague, duty sergeant, Helen Potter. He was fourteen years old. She spoke to him again.

15

"I don't suppose your mum knows you're out and about in this company, does she?"

George looked down at the pavement in silence.

"Well?" Rosie pushed. "And you know she and your dad are going through hell right now with your little brother being ill. Why are you out here on the streets?"

The boy just shrugged his shoulders.

"And what about you, young man?" said Rosie to the other boy. "What's your name?"

"Aiden," said the boy, still looking down.

"Aiden who?"

"Aiden Gallagher."

"And where do you live?"

Rosie took out her notepad and wrote down his address.

"Okay," she said. "I'm going to be seeing you both again soon, you can count on that. But for now, you can go."

Without a second's hesitation they both turned around and took off, and were around the corner and out of sight in no time.

Rosie turned to the officers nearby. "Back in my day I wouldn't dare ride my bike in the dark without lights in front of coppers!"

The officers laughed and went back to their duties while Rosie reached into her pocket for her phone and dialled a number. After a few seconds, Masoud answered.

"Listen, Faz, that young lad is still alive, just. His name is Louie, at least it might be. He should be at hospital by now, can you arrange a guard? Twenty-four seven, please."

"Yes, boss," came the reply. "You think he'll be attacked again?"

"Maybe. Don't really know, it's just a hunch. I think whoever stabbed him didn't want him to wake up. Oh, and is Helen still there?"

"Don't know, I'll check."

As the phone went silent for a while, Rosie watched the uniformed officers cordon off the crime scene. Attempted murder was a serious offence, so an investigation was about to get underway.

"Boss?" Masoud was back on the line.

"Yes, Faz, I'm here."

"Helen left about an hour ago."

"Okay," said Rosie looking at her watch. "I'll catch her tomorrow. See you later, Faz."

Rosie placed her phone in her pocket. The time was six fifty-five on an unseasonally cold evening in March. She pondered whether to call round to see Helen Potter or wait until morning. As Helen's youngest son Jack, only seven years old, had recently been diagnosed with acute myeloid leukaemia, Rosie felt she could wait until morning. The last thing Helen needed right then was a problem with her other son, but this couldn't be ignored. She would wait until morning, but there was no doubt that George would have to face questions, whether he was the son of a friend and colleague or not.

Rosie left the uniforms to deal with the crime scene, got into her car, and headed for home.

3

OCG boss Brian Hazell was pacing up and down the private bar area over the top of his club in Manchester. Something was bothering him, and he needed to think.

At the far end of the bar sat one of his trusted enforcers, a large man sporting multicoloured spiky hair, the most prominent colour being bright mauve. He had delivered the bad news to Hazell.

"How the fuck could this happen, Tommy?" snapped Hazell as he ran his left hand over his head, the short, spiky silver hair tickling his palm. In his right hand was the familiar sight of a cigarette, from which he took a long drag before continuing. "When we decide to terminate one of the runners, the whole fucking point is that we do it properly. We're professionals. First of all, we make sure the little fucker's dead, then we leave no clues behind. It's all got to be done under the radar. So, what the fuck happened?"

"The lad bottled it, boss," said Tommy.

"Wasn't he trained how to do this? Didn't he understand what would happen if he failed?"

"He was well trained, boss. And he knew what would happen if he failed. Whacko clearly explained what he'd do to his kid sister if he fucked up."

"So why didn't he do it?"

"He got scared and rushed it. We thought he had the bollocks for it, but he didn't. Sorry, boss. At least he didn't leave the blade at the scene; he lost it just as I told him."

"What about the gear? Did he empty the kid's pockets and get everything he was carrying?"

"No, boss."

"For fuck's sake!" shouted Hazell. "Tommy, that means the cops will find the drugs on him, and he might have written down the place he was taking them to. What gear was he delivering?"

"Cocaine."

"And where was he taking it?"

"An address in Harrogate town centre."

"Shit! So, we must assume the boy wrote down the address, which the cops will find along with the coke. Am I right?"

"Yes, boss."

"The lad has failed on an epic scale. The cops will visit the buyer who is bound to supply the phone number, which means we have to shut it down immediately. At least he got rid of the knife."

"Yes, boss, the knife is gone. As for the other lad, do you want me to get someone to the hospital to finish him off?"

"Not yet, it's too risky at the moment, but we will need to deal with young Louie if he recovers. He knows far too much, which is why I couldn't let him go back to mummy."

Hazell inhaled more nicotine as he paced back along the bar. As he turned back, he exhaled a large cloud of smoke before continuing.

"Look, Tommy, I'm not happy with how it's going in Harrogate. I think we need someone else to take over that place. Someone who can both deal with the lad if he wakes up, and make a success of things going forward. Who can we send?"

"How about Spike?"

"Yeah, Spike," answered Hazell, taking another drag on his cigarette while thinking it through. "That's a great shout, Tommy. I've been a bit worried about Spike lately, but it was him who supplied that kid and sent him to Harrogate in the first place. Maybe going over there is just what he needs, a new challenge, a chance to impress me once again, just like the old days. He'll deal with any problems with Louie and can build things up over there for us. Can you get him to come and see me?"

"Will do, boss."

"And tell me again about those two other lads?"

"First one's young Aiden, a good lad. A bit cheeky, but he's got a future. We took him out of Blackpool a while ago. Whacko took a shine to him, which is why we took him to Harrogate, well out of the way."

"Yeah, I remember. Whack's fondness for men, young boys included, is gonna be the undoing of him one day, you mark my words. If he ever lets it cause damage to business, I'll be ordering you to shoot him. Anyway, what about the other lad?"

"Yeah, George. He's a different story. Turns out he's the son of a copper over there."

"No shit."

"Yeah, no shit. He kept that quiet. When they were at the scene, the detective there recognised him. Young

Aiden told me that George has a younger brother who's poorly."

"How poorly?"

"Very poorly. He says it's leukaemia."

"That is very poorly. Nonetheless, this is all too awkward for my liking, Tommy. We need to do something about young George. What does he know?"

"Nothing, boss. Apart from knowing where the trap house is, he's been in the dark. We had plans for him, he showed promise, but he knows fuck all."

"That's good, the last thing we wanna do is knock off a cop's kid. Can you imagine the hassle that'd cause? If all he knows about is the trap house, we're moving out of there anyway. We can let him go home and make sure he doesn't come back."

"I can do that, boss. And he doesn't have a clue where we're going."

"Yeah, that's good, Tommy. Never forget, we always move on regularly. Never get sloppy with stuff like that, or someone will notice and get the law involved."

"I get it, boss. We're moving in a couple of days."

"Good, so tell the boy to fuck off back to his mum and don't come back. Make sure to scare the living shit out of him, so he won't think about making any contact with us again. After that we can move everything to the new location."

"I'll get rid of him tomorrow."

Hazell sucked on his cigarette once again while thinking. An idea had occurred to him.

"Hang on, Tommy," he said looking back at the enforcer. "On second thoughts, I wonder if there's an opportunity here. I think I might go to Harrogate tomorrow, take Spike with me, so he can get started over there. I don't wanna meet this kid with a poorly brother, but I've got an idea I want to explore. Can you fix it so I can get a look at his phone? Without him seeing me, of course."

"I'm sure Freddy can fix it, boss," said Tommy. "No problem."

"Good. And make sure he knows how to get into it, yeah?"

"I'll get on it now."

"Great. So, get hold of Spike, will you? Get him to me tonight. Tell him he's having a party here at the club, and the boss has got good news for him."

"Will do."

"And as for the lad who didn't finish Louie off and completely fucked up, we'll collect him tomorrow and get rid of him."

***

Rosie's daughter, eleven-year-old Sophie, was the apple of her eye. Although diagnosed with Down's syndrome shortly after birth, the bond between mother and daughter had been firm and unbreakable from day one. As Rosie pulled into the driveway, Sophie's smiling face was beaming at her from the lounge window. By the time she had got out and locked her car, Sophie had run out of the front door and jumped into the loving embrace of her mother.

"Hello, darling," said Rosie. "How's your day been?"

"Good, Mummy. I got a star today in class for getting good marks."

"Oh, wow! That's amazing. Take me inside and tell me all about it, it's too cold out here."

As soon as Rosie had closed the front door, little Sophie began telling all about her great day at school. Rosie's mother, Alison appeared from the kitchen.

"Didn't she do well?" said Rosie to her mother.

"She's been buzzing all evening. Couldn't wait for you to come home to tell you. What was the delay?"

"Oh, it was just an unfortunate incident on the edge of town," Rosie answered, not wishing to go into detail in the company of Sophie. "I left other officers on the scene to deal with it. So, what's for tea?"

"Granny's making spaghetti Bolognese," said Sophie, still bouncing up and down with excitement.

"Ooh, my favourite," said Rosie. "When will it be ready?"

"Ten minutes," said Alison.

"Okay then, let me get changed and we'll eat."

4

OCG boss Brian Hazell owned many businesses and properties around the country, most of which were based in or around his hometown of Manchester. Some of them were successful enterprises, some not so, but they all gave credible cover for his real money-making operations: the supply of illicit drugs, prostitution, high-level fraud, and theft. The list was extensive.

One of his enterprises was a bar situated close to the city centre, frequented mainly by businessmen and women during weekdays, until a younger clientele took over mid-evening and into the night. On the floor immediately above the hustle and bustle of the large bar was Brian Hazell's private bar and lounge area. Only those who could get past his fearsome private guards had access upstairs, meaning that admission could only be gained with Hazell's invitation, or in many cases, his summons.

On that evening, Hazell was sitting at the end of his long private bar, enjoying his whisky and a cigarette while waiting for his guest to arrive. He took a long drag while pondering over exactly what he was going to say and how he was going to say it.

As he blew out a large cloud of smoke and watched it disperse, he heard a loud noise from below. Hazell smiled as he envisioned the scene of another drunk fool making trouble, only to be confronted by the swift arrival of his large bouncers. Whoever it was would soon find themselves thrown out onto the street, with bumps and scars for souvenirs. Or perhaps it was once again an idiot thinking he could come upstairs to explore, and simply brush aside the man-mountain in his way. If so, he too would soon be outside, wondering why he was lying on the pavement with scrapes and bruises.

A door opened at the far end and two of his men arrived, accompanied by the person he was waiting for. He looked over and watched the young man enter, eyes wide at what he saw as he looked around. Sean McKenzie, who went by the street name "Spike", had never been invited upstairs before. The look on his face indicated that he was excited, honoured, and somewhat awestruck to be there. Hazell waved him over and dismissed the men.

"Come over here and sit down, Spike," he said. "Let's get you a drink."

Spike walked over and sat down on a bar stool next to Hazell.

"What can I get you, son?"

"Wouldn't say no to a beer," said Spike, pointing at the lager of his choice.

Hazell nodded at his private barman who began pouring into a pint glass. Spike watched in silence as the barman filled the glass and placed it down in front of him.

"Cheers, Spike," said Hazell.

"Cheers, boss," said Spike as he lifted the glass and took a long swig.

"Not a bad gaff I've got myself here, is it, Spike?"

"It's amazing, boss."

"Yeah, it is. This is where I like to hang out, and where I make plans for the business. Where I make my moves, know what I mean, Spike?"

"Yeah, boss. I get it."

"It's about respect, son. And fear. If I ever lose respect, I'm finished. People need to know that if they cross me, they're dead. Otherwise, they'd kill me and take over everything I've worked for. Know what I mean?"

"Er, yes, boss." Spike's pulse thrummed in his wrists. Had Hazell discovered that he'd been helping himself to the goods and cash?

"That's why those who opposed me have been crushed, Spikey boy. I've seen to it that many have disappeared without trace."

Spike's heart pounded in his chest as he took another hasty gulp of his lager while Hazell continued.

"You did a great job in Bradford, Spike. I was well impressed. Shame you had to leave, as a matter of fact."

"Yeah." Spike laughed nervously. "That wanker over there was gunning for me."

"Khan."

"Yeah, Adeel Khan. He wanted me dead, and you too from what I heard."

"I know, I heard that too. As a matter of fact, the bastard took a shot at me. I'll have him for that one of these days. But, like I say, you did a good job. Hasn't gone quite so well in Blackburn though, why's that?"

"It's been slow, boss. But it's coming together. I recruited some kids over there and we're starting to rock 'n' roll."

"Yeah, that's good. But I've been worried about you, Spike."

"Why's that, boss?"

"I want results, and I don't think you've been on it lately. Should I be worried?"

"Not at all. Just give me a bit more time and I'll show you what I can do."

"Okay, Spike. But listen, I've got a better idea."

Spike paused a few seconds while he thought about what Hazell had said. Did this mean he was going to make him redundant? Which meant have him bumped off? No way, not after his success in Bradford. Surely the boss would stick with him. Or, more worryingly, perhaps Hazell had discovered he'd been syphoning off some of the cash and drugs lately. That would result in his execution, without a doubt. He'd be one of those who'd disappeared without trace.

"A better idea?" he said. "What do you mean?"

"I think you need a new challenge, Spike."

"A new challenge? What sort of new challenge?"

"Stop worrying, Spike. This is good news, son. A promotion."

Spike breathed a sigh of relief. Perhaps the boss hadn't found out he had been stealing.

"A promotion?"

"Yeah, a new challenge, Spike. I need someone with your talent to take over and build some real success in a new town. A great place it is too, the best assignment of all."

"Where's that, boss?"

"Harrogate."

"Harrogate?" said Spike, a little louder than he intended. "Boss, I hate Yorkshire, can't someone else go there?"

"I don't have anyone else of your calibre, Spike. You're the man for the job. I want Harrogate to be the jewel in the crown, so to speak, and I want you to do it for me."

"Oh, okay. So, when do I go?"

"Tomorrow. I'll take you myself. While we're on our way, I'll explain exactly what's been happening there and what I need you to do straight away. We'll leave early in the morning; you can stay here tonight."

"Stay here? At the club?"

"Yeah, here at the club. We've got plenty of things here that'll keep you entertained for the night. Perhaps you might enjoy the company of a lady?"

"Sounds good to me, boss."

"Then drink up, Spike. And I'll get one of the lads to get you fixed up."

"Wow. Thanks, boss."

"You're welcome, son. Have fun tonight; tomorrow you start work."

As he watched Spike finish his beer and follow the man out of the bar, an excited smile on his face in anticipation of the treats he was about to receive, Hazell lit another cigarette and turned his thoughts onto more important matters. Harrogate. How was he going to give himself an edge over there? What could he do to get himself what he called an *unfair advantage*?

Ideally, he would like someone on the team at Harrogate police station in his pocket. An insider. An informant. Like many OCG bosses, he had bent police officers on the payroll, which was an effective way of keeping clear of those seeking to bring him to justice.

Some police officers, while being looked after with regular *benefits* such as lots of cash, lavish gifts, free sex according to their preferred desires, whatever else would *float their boat*, or a combination of such inducements, provided Hazell with information. If, for example, a raid was going to happen on one of Hazell's properties or businesses, advance notice was given. If an officer or a team of detectives were investigating something that might be of interest to Hazell, again he was informed. Or if Hazell wanted specific information about something or someone, all he had to do was push the right buttons.

His informers were always kept *topped up* with whatever took their fancy, making sure they stayed close and wanted more. They were well and truly in his pocket, and once they were in, he had them for life. He knew, as did they, that any step out of line and their lives would be ruined.

Hazell, being cunning and clever, used all such information to his advantage, and had kept himself, his businesses, and his vast profits, at least one step ahead of the law for many years.

The problem was, he had no such informers east of the Pennines, nor did he have any idea who to approach with an offer they, hopefully, couldn't refuse. His mind turned to one of his bent coppers in Manchester, a detective sergeant that Hazell knew from previous conversations had regular contact with cops from other police forces across the North of England. Perhaps he might be able to suggest some names and provide contact details. Risky, but done in the right way by targeting an Achilles' heel, a chink in their armour, he might be able to gain entry and get someone useful on board.

Hazell composed a message on WhatsApp to his contact in the Greater Manchester police force.

> **Hope you and the missus enjoyed your fancy holiday I paid for! I need a reliable source over at Harrogate, and I need it asap. Have a good think – who do you know over there who might be useful. Tell me about them, what makes them tick, how can I get them to bite. I need this to happen yesterday! BTW, that young blonde Russian bird with the big tits, Anya has been asking about you… once you've helped get me a face in Harrogate, get yourself over to my gaff and put a smile on her face!**

Hazell read the message through one last time, smiled at the reference to the Russian girl, then hit the send button before upending his glass to finish the whisky, savouring the burning sensation at the back of his throat. The barman was ready to fix a refill.

As he lit another cigarette, his phone buzzed on the bar top. He picked it up and read the message.

> **Leave it with me. I know many cops at Harrogate and can think of 2 or 3 who might have good reason**

to play ball. Will send details in the morning, with phone numbers. Will be over to see Anya sometime soon. Can't wait to get my mitts on those tits!!

"Yeah, I know you can't," muttered Hazell to himself, smiling. "You dirty bastard. Amazing how easy it is to get things done, if you know how. And besides, what do you do when you need to know something? You ask a policeman, of course."

***

A couple of young ladies, no more than twenty years old, staggered away from a late-night bar in Parliament Street in Harrogate, heading for the taxi rank. They had enjoyed their evening, drinking and chatting, but had overindulged a little. After flirting with the barman and a couple of patrons, they realised it was late and decided it was time to leave.

As they passed a shop doorway on a quiet part of the street, giggling as they held on to each other, a young boy on a bike with his dark hoodie down over a baseball cap approached them.

"Hello, ladies," he said. "Do you need anything this evening?"

The girls stopped and looked at the lad.

"Ooh, I say," said one of the ladies. "What kind of things do you have in mind?" Her friend giggled some more.

"Well," said the confident lad. "If you play your cards right this could be your lucky night."

Both girls erupted in laughter.

"How old are you?" asked the same lady.

"Old enough to give you a good night. Shame my mate George isn't here, but never mind. I'll have to manage on my own."

More hysterics from the ladies, before one of them spoke again.

"Come on then, we're getting bored now. What do you want from us?"

"Well, I've got some gear that you're gonna like. And if that's not good enough for you I can get some more. What do you want?"

"What's your name then?" asked the same girl. "And how old are you?"

"My name's Casanova, and I'm twenty-five."

Both girls burst out laughing once again.

"You look bloody good for twenty-five, Casanova."

"That's cos I take the right pills every day. I've got some here for you, if you like."

"No thanks, Casanova," said the other young lady. "Maybe some other time."

"Okay, so give me your phone numbers so we can keep you up to date with what goodies we've got."

"Just fuck off now," shouted one of ladies followed by a hiccup. "We're going home now."

"Tell you what," said the boy, persevering. "If you give me your phone numbers, I'll give you something for free, right now."

"What you got for free?"

"How about a feel-good pill?" said the lad, holding up a packet containing an ecstasy tablet. "One free pill for each number."

The young ladies looked at each other.

"What do you think?" asked one to the other. She was struggling to stand up, let alone think straight.

"I don't see why not," said the other, who was even more inebriated. "A freebie."

The boy told them the number of the mobile phone he was holding, and they each sent him a text. When he had received them, one from each lady, he handed over two packets.

"There you go, ladies," he said. "Enjoy the rest of your night."

Young Aiden Gallagher pedalled his bike away, leaving the giggling ladies to themselves.

"That's nine numbers from new punters I've got tonight," he said to himself as he made his way back to the trap house. "Freddy will be pleased."

That was one way that drug gangs acquired a database of potential customers. Whenever they needed to ditch a burner phone, which they did regularly, they would send a batch text from a new phone, informing customers of the new number to use whenever they wanted fresh supplies.

County lines were well organised and managed operations.

5

Thursday

Life at the Potter household had got distinctly complicated since seven-year-old Jack, the youngest of Helen's two sons, had been diagnosed with myeloid leukaemia. Understandably, it had been a hammer blow for her and her husband Gavin. Everything had been turned upside down as Jack began treatment while they tried to keep up with their careers.

Helen Potter, a well-respected and hard-working duty sergeant at Harrogate police station, had been desperate to keep up with the day-to-day demands her job threw at her. The same applied to Gavin, an architect. However, the attention that they usually gave to their older son, fourteen-year-old George, inevitably waned, diminishing to the point where he was left to his own devices more or less on a daily basis.

As Helen fussed around getting Jack ready while trying to eat some cold toast, George, while remaining virtually invisible, as was usual, had got himself ready and was about to leave. As he was heading for the door, his mother finally noticed him.

"Bye, sweetheart," she shouted just as the front door closed behind him. "Have a good day at school."

"Yeah, right," he mumbled sarcastically.

He grabbed his bike out of the garage, hopped on, and was gone.

He stopped round the corner and looked at his phone. He disabled the tracking app the family used, as he did on a regular basis, just in case his parents actually bothered to look, then continued on his way. School was the last place on his list of places he intended to be on that morning.

Young George was more interested in adding cash to the pot he had been accumulating in recent days and weeks. His friendship with Aiden Gallagher, a fifteen-year-old lad that his parents would certainly not approve of, had brought him fun, freedom and money.

Good money.

Real money.

His new life was a blast. Who needed school?

***

As head of Operation Caterpillar, Rosie led a team investigating crimes relating to county lines, predominately in the local area. She was also involved with cases in other areas of North Yorkshire from time to time, and had to liaise with officers across the country, as the fight against Serious and Organised Crime (SOC) was a matter of national concern. Regular contact with the Regional Organised Crime Units (ROCU) and the National Crime Agency (NCA) was also essential. ROCU managed cross-border SOC, seeking to remove the advantage criminals used to have by crossing territorial boundaries. The NCA was a nationwide force fighting SOC. Naturally, regular communication and cooperation was essential to ensure that a unified and organised approach was made nationwide to create an effective fight against the scourge of organised crime.

"It's like trying to sweep runny shit uphill, Faz," said Rosie as they both sat down at a table in a quaint, privately owned coffee shop in the town centre.

"So you keep saying, boss," replied Masoud laughing.

"Well, it is. The harder you push, the quicker the soft and smelly stuff rolls back down. Every time we put one drug pusher away, another thug arrives to take over. There's a conveyor belt somewhere churning out these bastards and dumping them on our streets. Each time we get a result, we have to start again."

"Excuse me, boss," said Masoud as he picked up his phone. He took a call.

Of all the team of officers and support staff, Rosie relied on Detective Sergeant Fazli Masoud and two detective constables known as "the gendarmes" the most. A couple of years previously, DCs John French and Maxime Leblanc had been assigned to her team and she quickly discovered that despite Max Leblanc having French parents, he was in fact born in London, within the sound of Bow bells, making him not just a true cockney, but a French cockney, much to Rosie's amusement. Being paired up to work with a detective by the name of French was pure poetry for Rosie, so she came up with the moniker "les gendarmes", which morphed into "the gendarmes", and took no time at all to become known to all at the station.

While the gendarmes were back at the station, Rosie had arranged to meet Masoud in town for a coffee before going to the station, and Masoud was more than happy to oblige. They had found seats by the window in a coffee shop in Oxford Street in the centre of town, which happened to have a good view of some of the nearby shops and establishments, including a large McDonald's fast-food restaurant.

Rosie finally sampled her coffee as Masoud finished a phone call. She was a little disappointed with it and placed her cup down in disgust.

"Honestly, Faz," she said. "This coffee is as weak as a fortnight. I might have to get another."

Masoud replaced his phone in his pocket while laughing at her humorous comment, not for the first time, and certainly not for the last.

"That was Max," said Masoud. "The young lad is still critical, but stable. The doctors are more optimistic than they were last night."

"That's great news, Faz. I didn't have much hope for him when he was lying in the street. Any idea who he is?"

"Not for sure, but Max says that a lady in Blackburn reported her young lad missing a couple of months ago. His name is Louie Bryant. Officers over there have sent photos over so we can ID him."

"Now, that is interesting. When can we get someone to the hospital with a photo?"

"Max is on his way right now. But what's also interesting is that young Louie was carrying cocaine along with a note with an address on it. It's a local address, could be where he was going to deliver the drugs to."

"Could be, Faz. We'll check it out this morning. But if the gang decided to kill this young lad, which it looks like they did, why wouldn't they empty his pockets?"

"Panic, fear, maybe the perp was disturbed."

"Whatever, Faz, I'm pleased the mistake was made as it gives us more to go on."

"Yes, boss. And what will happen to this young man? Assuming he survives of course."

"What will happen to him? I hope he gets the help he needs."

"Me too, boss, even though he's been delivering drugs."

"I know that, and yes he's been breaking the law. All the kids involved in this awful business are breaking the law. But we need to start thinking about how we treat them; do we look at them as villains or victims?"

"Yes, exactly," said Masoud nodding his head in agreement, his dark brown eyes darting around while in thought. "We've spoken about this many times before. How many of them are forced into doing this?"

"Lots of them. Maybe all of them. It's a form of child abuse, in my opinion. These kids are victims of this business too, and I hope the young lad gets all the help he needs. And the rest of them too."

"Absolutely, boss. I guess that applies to Helen's kid too, eh? I bet you couldn't believe your eyes when you saw him at the scene last night."

"I was nearly in shock, Faz," said Rosie as she let out a long sigh of despair. She used her fingers to brush some hair behind her ear before continuing. "Once the penny dropped and I realised who it was, I had to shake my head to make sure I wasn't dreaming."

"Young George Potter, eh?" said Masoud, deep in thought while his fingers massaged his black well-manicured beard. "Who would've thought?"

"I know, what with poor Jack going through the mill with his leukaemia, the last thing Helen needs is me having a chat this morning to give her the good news that George has become an apprentice gangster."

"Are you going to tell her?"

"Of course I'm going to tell her," Rosie stated as she took her eyes away from the activity out in the street to look directly at her colleague. "How can I not tell her?"

"Yes, of course. I just thought you might do something to get him away from the gangs first."

"And how exactly am I going to do that?"

"I don't know. Suppose I hadn't thought it through. Of course you must tell her."

"Exactly, Faz. Helen and her husband need to deal with this themselves, at home. I can help, though I've no idea how, but I'm willing to offer my assistance."

They both watched a lady walk slowly from the direction of Cheltenham Crescent towards a bench right outside the north-facing side of McDonald's. She wore a tatty blue anorak with a tear on the right elbow, filthy looking black leggings and had old dirty trainers on her feet. Her hair hadn't been washed in a while, nor had it been brushed. She had piercings in her ears and nose, and what looked to Rosie like another on her eyebrow. The lady's eyes were darting around nervously, apparently looking for something or someone. She sat down on the bench.

"We're just on doubling down on watching these kids, boss," said Masoud, who had also noticed the lady. "So, I wonder if George can help in some way. Maybe to locate where they operate from."

"I know. That's what I've been thinking. I let him go last night, telling the officers on scene to leave the kids to me, that I'd handle them. And ideally, I'd be talking with Helen right now, explaining what I've found out about George and working on ways to help, all the while keeping it well away from our investigation. But having slept on it, we just can't let this go. Not such a vital source of information as a kid who must know something that can help us."

"So, what's the plan?"

"I'm going to see Helen as soon as I get back, tell her about George and take it from there. But I will have to go and see the boy as soon as I can, which means today, no matter what Helen wants or is going through. And the other lad too, what was his name, Aiden Gallagher, I think."

"We've got plenty to get on with, boss."

"Yes, we have. But I'd still like to have a half-decent coffee before I leave for the station, if that's okay. And I wanted to talk to you about this part of town. The intel we've been getting is that these kids on bikes have been seen a lot around McDonald's, right here in front of us. I'm thinking of organising some better surveillance. The CCTV around here hasn't been of much help so far."

Masoud nodded in agreement. Rosie was about to take her cup to get a better alternative when movement outside caught her eye. A youngster on a bike appeared from Cambridge Street, zooming around the corner before coming to a halt next to the scruffy lady on the bench.

"Hello," said Rosie, replacing her cup on the table. "What have we got here?"

"A kid on a bike. Could be making a delivery."

"Yeah, which is exactly why I wanted to come here for coffee, to have a look around and see if it's worth organising surveillance. Looks like it is, Faz. Although I didn't think deliveries would happen this early in the day."

The kid on the bike grabbed something from the lady while at the same time handing her a packet before shooting off in the other direction. In seconds he was gone, but the lady, who didn't have the advantage of transport to provide a quick getaway, stood up while pocketing the packet and began to stroll away back towards Cheltenham Crescent.

"Faz!" Rosie barked. "Go and get that lady."

Masoud was out of the shop in an instant, followed by Rosie who was regretting not having had any coffee. She would have to get another at the station later. She paced up the street and around the corner, where Masoud had the lady with him. In his hand was a packet containing something that looked distinctly illegal. The woman was about to be chauffeur driven to the station for a chat.

6

Sean McKenzie, known to many as Spike, was sitting alongside Brian Hazell in the back seat of a large black Mercedes. Hazell's trusted driver, Jimmy, was taking them over the Pennines on the M62 heading for Yorkshire. The nasty thug had been trying to sleep off the effects of the all-night session of sex and drugs, all provided at Brian Hazell's expense. The two Scandinavian prostitutes he had chosen, had given him the best night of his life. He had been thoroughly taken care of in ways many never get to experience, all the while enjoying what seemed an endless supply of cocaine. Spike still had a smile on his face, although he was finding it hard to stay awake.

"So, young Spike," said the talkative Brian Hazell, once again preventing him from drifting off to sleep. "You enjoyed yourself last night, eh?"

"Yes, boss. Thank you very much."

"You're welcome, son. Just don't ever forget where your loyalties should be."

"Of course," replied Spike, quickly looking at Hazell, suddenly alert. Was the boss suggesting something? "No one is more loyal than me, boss."

"That's what I wanna hear, Spike. Quid pro quo, innit."

"Eh?"

"Quid pro quo. You scratch my back, I'll scratch yours. You do what I want and what I say, and I'll look after you. Catch my drift?"

"Yeah, I get you."

Spike relaxed; Hazell hadn't discovered his misdemeanours, and he was being taken to Harrogate to lead the drugs gang, and not about to be used as a foundation for a new bridge somewhere. He rubbed his shaved head, then felt the mark of his latest tattoo, a delightful looking spider behind his right ear. It went nicely with the swastika on the left side of his head.

"I'm not often out on site, Spike. These days I leave all that to my assistants, you know, Tommy mainly, or Whacko. You've met Whacko, haven't you?"

"Yeah, I met Whacko a couple of times. Nice bloke."

"Yeah, right," said Hazell laughing. "Not what I'd call a nice bloke. In fact, I pity anyone who gets on the wrong side of Whack. Anyway, I digress. I was saying, I don't go out on site much anymore, but when I do I'm not usually happy going in one of the limos." Hazell paused while sweeping his hand around, a gesture inviting Spike to take another good look at the luxurious interior of his top-of-the-range Mercedes. "Can't drum it into you enough, Spikey boy. We gotta keep under the radar in this business, know what I mean? Don't attract too much attention, blend in, be the grey man, don't stay in one place too long, don't repeat habits and movements. Get my drift, Spike?"

"Yes, boss."

"Yet here we are, driving towards your new territory in a fancy motor. Thing is, Spike, it's more important that I give the right impression when we get there, know what I mean? I want everyone there to know who's boss. What would it look like if I turned up in a beat-up old Ford, or whatever? I need respect, Spike. That's how this all works, respect. And fear. My reputation is everything. Don't want any juniors getting big ideas, thinking they can take over. Know what I mean?"

"Too right, boss."

"You wouldn't ever think about doing something stupid like that, would you, Spike?"

"Like what, boss?" said Spike, all thoughts about whether Hazell knew something about his indiscretions returning in a flash.

"Like dreaming of taking over. Helping yourself to some of the business, or some of the merchandise, or some of the cash."

"Wouldn't dream of it, boss." Spike was on high alert once again. Maybe he *was* on the way to being fitted with a concrete overcoat after all. He didn't fancy being handed a different assignment, such as holding up a new flyover. But then why would the boss have treated him to such a good night? "Whatever you want me to do, boss, I'm on it. You know that."

"I know, Spike, I know. Just that lately I've been wondering if you've had your eye off the ball, know what I mean? I need you back to your best, son. That's why this new job over in Harrogate is perfect for you. And for me. It's a great opportunity for both of us. I need you to deliver, Spike."

"You can count on me, boss."

"Good lad, Spike. That's what I wanna hear. So, the first thing we gotta do when we get to Harrogate is move our trap house. It was going to happen next week, but last night I changed my mind and brought it forward. We're doing it today. Tommy's got Freddy to organise it. You see, Spike old son, you'll learn many things from me, but none more important than the importance of keeping on the move. You know why that's important?"

"Because that way we keep ahead of the pack."

"Exactly. So, yesterday I ordered that a young runner be terminated. You might remember him, young Louie. He was becoming a pain in the arse, wanting to go home to his mummy. I couldn't have any shit like that, so he had to go, know what I mean? Anyway, we sent a couple more kids to the scene to check out the success of the hit, but they got stopped and questioned. The detective asking them questions recognised one of them, turns out that he's the son of a local copper. Fucking shame actually, he would've been useful that kid. We were about to send him away to do some running for us over at Preston. Now we'll have to let him go; I don't want his mum and her mates coming for us, all for the sake of a little boy. We can get plenty of kids just like him, so he can go. The point is, we don't want him identifying the trap house, do we?"

"No, boss. That wouldn't be good."

"Quite right. At least not until we've already gone. Which is why we're moving today."

"Okay, boss. So, what happened to the other kid?"

"What other kid?"

"Louie. Is he history?"

"No, he isn't. Which has fucking pissed me off no end, Spike. He's still alive apparently and kept under guard at the local hospital. I might be in touch with you about him as I want the job finished."

"You can count on me for that job, boss," said Spike with a huge grin.

"Yeah, I thought you might be interested in that assignment, Spikey boy. I'm gonna have to think about that. I might prefer to send someone over to do it. Anyway, you look like you could do with a nap. Get your head down, I need you on the ball later."

"Okay, boss."

Spike welcomed the suggestion and leant his head back against his rolled-up hoodie and closed his eyes.

7

Rosie held as tight as she could as her dear friend and colleague sobbed her heart out, letting it all go as she hugged Rosie with all her might. Sergeant Helen Potter had been strong, stoic, and determined to perform her duties to her usual high standards despite the hell she had been going through.

When Helen's son, seven-year-old Jack, had been diagnosed with myeloid leukaemia, treatment had begun immediately. Although Jack was able to live a more or less normal life while undergoing treatment, the fact was that he had an uphill battle while he was fighting for his life. The last thing Helen needed was more bad news, so when Rosie had taken her into a private room and explained what she had seen the previous evening, it proved too much. She started shaking before erupting into floods of tears. All Rosie could do was hold her tight and wait a while before she could begin to assure her friend that between them they would work this one out.

Eventually Helen loosened her grip and stood back a little. Rosie handed her another tissue, which she gratefully accepted.

"Are you sure it was him, Rosie?" Helen asked while dabbing her eyes.

"I'm positive, sweetheart," Rosie replied, using a term of endearment she was well known for. She had little time for tedious rules and political correctness. "He was with another lad called Aiden Gallagher. Do you know him?"

"Never heard of him. He told me the other day he's been hanging out with new friends lately, so maybe Aiden is one of them."

"That's a bad sign. New friends is a sign of potential trouble with drug gangs. You know that, Helen."

"I know. I've just not had my eye on things. Come to think of it, George has been buying things, new clothes, trainers, a fancy phone, and I've no idea where he got the money from. I suppose I've been ignoring the obvious, haven't I?"

"Yes, clearly you have, but in your case it's understandable. So, we've got to do something to help him, yeah? Easier said than done, but we can do it. Do you know where George is today?"

"At school, I hope."

Helen started crying again, the emotions all coming to the surface at once. Clearly Helen had been focusing on Jack and his issues while still insisting on doing her job, and refusing to accept any compassionate leave, at least for the time being. Rosie had urged her to take time out, but Helen had insisted that life had to go on, which meant that she was going to do her job and do it well, like she always did. While Rosie always respected her choices and the way she was going about facing her challenges, it seemed that she had been paying little or no attention to Jack's older brother, who had managed to get into some bad company.

48

The sobbing stopped and Rosie spoke. "We're going to have to talk with George, you do understand that don't you, darling?"

"Yes, of course."

"But while doing what we have to do, I will always be here for you. I will help you get through this."

"Thank you, Rosie."

"Okay, sweetheart. So, tell me about how Jack's doing."

"Not too bad, but there's a long way to go. The NHS has been great; Jack's getting the best treatment available. Gav and I are also looking into private treatment, seeing if it might give Jack more chance of survival."

"That sounds expensive."

"It is, I'm afraid. But we'll do anything, even sell the house if it means keeping Jack with us."

"Oh my god, Helen. You're going to get me crying in a minute. Listen, maybe we can help here at the station. There are ways of raising funds: sponsored walks, marathons, coffee and cake mornings, things like that. There are lots of us who would help try to raise a few quid to help Jack."

"I know they would, but I hate to ask."

"Well, I'd love to ask! Leave it with me. I'll have a think about how we can organise something. But meanwhile we've got work to do, and you must start paying attention to George, yeah?"

"I know, I know. Gav and I haven't been there for him at all lately."

"Okay, I'm going to have to go and talk with George. If I can find him that is, and then tonight I can come round

49

and see you all. Maybe we can come up with ways to help. Is that a plan?"

"That's great, Rosie. Thank you."

The ladies hugged again before leaving the room and going their separate ways.

***

Rosie made her way across the police station as she wanted to listen in to the interview with the lady they had picked up earlier in town.

Joanne Chapman was a twenty-three-year-old addict who had ventured into town to collect her latest fix.

Rosie sat in a nearby room and tuned in to a live recording of the interview which had started a few minutes previously. Joanne looked dreadful: dirty, unkempt and scruffy. Rosie was pleased she wasn't sitting in the room. Next to Chapman was a duty solicitor, and across the table were DC John French and a colleague, a new detective to the North Yorkshire force, DC Rachel Sutherland.

"So, one more time, Joanne," said French. "How long have you been using that number to call for supplies?"

"Dunno, a month I suppose."

"A month. And what did you do before that?"

"I had another number."

"Another number, eh? So, what happened to that other number?"

"It stopped working."

"Then what?"

"I got the new number."

"From the same dealers?"

"No. This crowd were new. When I saw them, they insisted I get my gear from them."

"What happened to the previous suppliers?" asked French.

"They weren't in the picture anymore."

"How did you know they weren't in the picture?"

"Cos that's what the new bloke told me. He said his mates had taken over and I wasn't allowed to buy from them anymore."

"What was the name of this bloke?"

"I dunno. He never told me his name. He said that I wouldn't hear from him again, and that I had to use the phone to call, and someone would deliver the gear."

"And who would deliver the gear?"

"A kid did it."

"Which kid? The same kid?"

"Usually it was the same kid, yeah."

"What was his name?"

"I dunno. I only saw him for a few seconds every time. We never spoke."

"Okay, Joanne," said French in his gruff Yorkshire voice. "You're in trouble here, but what we really want is to get to the suppliers. I need you to tell me everything you know about them."

Rosie got up to leave, believing it to be a waste of time. She had found herself paying more attention to the new detective, Rachel Sutherland, an attractive, young Black officer, who seemed content to sit through much of the interview staring at her manicured nails. Rosie made a point to speak to Sutherland sometime soon, to ascertain exactly how serious she was about her career as a detective.

As for Chapman, it was clear that she either knew nothing at all about the suppliers, or if she did, she was too poorly to be of much use. If she needed a fix, it was likely she would be rattling soon, if not already. When withdrawal symptoms set in, Chapman would be unable to provide anything useful. Besides, they already had her phone, so they knew the number she'd been using to get her drugs.

The problem was that number had been shut down already, and Rosie reckoned she knew why. The gangsters had realised that the police would find a note on young Louie with an address, so would have immediately stopped using that particular number, which may well have been the same number Joanne was using. Another burner phone would be used, and the gangsters and runners would have already started communicating that new number to punters.

However, the phone number could still prove useful, as maybe they would be able to trace a location where it had been used. Masoud had been working on that, so Rosie left the room to go and find him.

Maybe, with a little luck for once, they could locate a premises where the thugs worked from and organise a raid.

Her thoughts were interrupted by the sound of her phone ringing. It was Max Leblanc.

"What've you got, Max?"

"Just got back from the hospital, boss. That kid is definitely Louie Bryant."

"Okay, can you call our colleagues over the Pennines with the news? They'll need to send someone round to let the lad's mother know what's happened."

"Will do."

Rosie replaced the phone in her pocket and paused to think. Not the best news for the poor mother, but at least he's alive, which means there's still hope. No doubt she'll be making her way over to see her son as soon as possible.

Rosie started to walk again, making her way to the incident room.

8

Brian Hazell looked down at the young lad, thinking carefully about the story the boy had just told him. They were standing in a scruffy, smelly lounge belonging to an old, lonely, and disabled lady who had been cuckooed. They'd taken over her home in exchange for free food and booze, along with serious threats should she decide to mention their presence to anyone. The base had been set up a couple of months before where the local handler and kids had hung out, and some of the drugs and cash had been stored.

Hazell had ordered a new place to be found; they'd been there too long already, and besides, he believed it had been compromised after the stabbing the evening before. The police would be there in due course, possibly soon.

Alongside Hazell stood Spike to one side, and on the other was the local handler, a man known by the street name 'Freddy'. Next to Freddy was the nervous figure of a young man called Jamie, who had been ordered to terminate young Louie the evening before. He was nervous because he knew he had messed up by not finishing the job off, along with failing to clear Louie's pockets. The old lady was in her bedroom where she'd been instructed to remain, and keeping her company was George Potter, who had been relieved of his mobile phone and ordered to stay with the lady until summoned. Hazell didn't want to meet George, nor did he want their discussion to be heard by the son of a police officer. But he did want to take a look at his phone.

"What's your name again, son?" Hazell asked the boy standing in front of him.

"Aiden."

"Okay, Aiden. So, one more time, you delivered to a lady in town this morning, a lady you've seen many times, but then she got lifted. Is that right?"

"Yeah. I shot away soon as we did the switch, but I doubled back and saw her with a man and a woman. I know they were cops, cos a police car arrived and took the lady away."

"She was arrested then?"

"Looked that way to me, yeah."

"Right," said Hazell, taking out a cigarette. "That means getting out of here is even more urgent. I'm taking a huge risk just being here, so we'll be away in a few minutes. The cops will take her phone and see she called our number. They'll then be able to locate where that number's been used, which is here. They'll be outside that door fucking soon."

As Hazell put the cigarette in his mouth and raised his lighter, young Aiden spoke again.

"Margaret doesn't like us smoking here, boss. Bad for her breathing."

"Who the fuck's Margaret?" shouted Hazell, making the kid jump.

"Er, the lady here," Aiden stammered while pointing towards the bedroom where the householder was situated.

Hazell turned to Spike and spoke again. "Can you believe what that kid just said, Spike?"

"No, boss. Never heard such bollocks."

"Well, fuck her," said Hazell talking to Aiden once again. "I'm in fucking charge here, you got that, kiddo?"

"Yes, sir," replied Aiden, watching Hazell fire up his cigarette and take a long drag.

"Right, good. So, young Aiden, where do you come from?"

"Blackpool."

"And how long have you been here?"

"A few weeks. A couple of months maybe."

"Well, Aiden, you need to move on. Spike here will walk you to the station and tell you where to go, and who to report to. It's not safe here anymore, so I'm having to start things again. You got that?"

"Yes, sir."

"And you too, Freddy. You're coming back with me."

"Why's that, boss?"

"Because Spike is taking over, as of right now."

"I thought I was doing okay, boss."

"Well, you thought wrong. Anyhow, we've been compromised here. Unless we start again with new faces we're fucked. Know what I mean? Anyway, I've got something else for you to do, you'll be starting there tonight. You got a problem with that?"

"Where am I going, boss?" said Freddy.

"Blackburn, where Spike just came from. Things are running nicely there, so there'll be no excuses for any fuckups. Understood?"

"Yes, boss."

"As for you, Jamie," said Hazell turning to the young man in the corner. "You really have made a bollocks of things."

"I'm sorry, boss," he said, close to tears.

"So, why the fuck didn't you finish him off?"

"I thought I had, boss. I stabbed him three times, deep cuts. I twisted the third one, just like Whacko and Tommy taught me. I can't believe he isn't dead."

"Well, he isn't dead. And to make matters worse, you failed to clear the lad. He had supplies, and even the fucking address where he was delivering to. How did that happen?"

"I thought I heard someone coming, boss. So I shot off."

"Sounds like bollocks to me. More like you fucking forgot."

"Sorry, boss."

"Yeah, well, we'll have to see what we're gonna do with you, Jamie. You're coming back with me too. Tommy and Whack are gonna give you some, er, more training."

Jamie didn't like the sound of that, but didn't dare to say anything further.

"And finally, there's young George," Hazell stated. "I need to send him home."

"Can't we use him somewhere else?" asked Spike.

"I'd love to," Hazell answered. "I've heard good things about him. But I don't want to attract any more attention from the cops, yeah? I can't even have him terminated and dumped somewhere; we just don't need the shitstorm we'd get from the pigs. Best that we tell him to fuck off home, and we'll have to be nice to him as he might very well be asked questions about us. Bad enough he's been on a few deliveries, and he knows what's been going on, which he might tell the cops about. But I can't have him saying anything else, stuff that might cause me a problem. So, we need to be firm with him about not contacting us again, but don't threaten him too much. Anyway, before we go, let me see his phone."

Spike handed the phone over.

"Did he show you how to get into it, Spike?"

"Yeah, I've just done it for you."

Hazell studied the phone and scrolled through, examining the data. Whenever he found something that might be of interest, he used his own phone to photograph the screen. After repeating that exercise a few times, he wiped the phone clean with a handkerchief and handed the phone back to Spike.

"Okay," he said before pointing at Jamie. "Come on, kiddo, let's get the fuck out of here. You too, Freddy. My limo's a few streets away; didn't want to draw attention to us by leaving it outside, know what I mean? While we're walking, I'll call Jimmy to come and pick us up."

Hazell then turned to Spike.

"Spike, you're in charge now," he said sternly. "Turn this place into big profits, yeah? Make me proud, son. First thing you gotta do is give young George his phone back and tell him to clear off, then get Aiden to the station.

After that, go and check out the new trap house that Freddy organised. Don't let me down, Spike."

"You got it, boss."

Hazell, Freddy and the petrified young Jamie made their way out and were gone.

Spike went through to the bedroom and collected George Potter.

***

After wiping the phone clean for fingerprints once again, Spike had handed the phone back to George and brought him into the dingy lounge.

"So, you're George then, are you, son?"

"Yes, sir," replied George. He was shaking with nerves. Spike was a scary looking man, able to strike fear into most grown adults, let alone a young schoolboy.

"Don't be scared, Georgie boy. We've heard good things about you, and we know you've done nothing wrong, apart from one thing; you should've told us your mum's in the police force, yeah?"

George remained silent, staring down at the filthy carpet.

"Yeah, George?" Spike repeated.

"Yes, sir," said the startled George. "I'm sorry, sir."

"Alright, Georgie boy. I'm not mad at you. I can understand why you didn't say anything about your mum. But now we know, do you understand why I can't let you hang out with us anymore?"

"Yeah, I suppose."

"Good lad. Anyway, your mate Aiden here, is going away to work in Bradford, and no, you can't go with him.

I want you to go back home and back to school. Back to your family. You got that?"

"Okay."

"I mean it, George. You can't come here anymore. I'm going to let you keep whatever you have, and the boss is giving you some extra cash too. In return for that, I want you to do something for me. If you're asked by your mum, or any other copper, you say nothing about us, yeah? And nothing about meeting me. Can you do that for me?"

"Okay."

"And nothing about what you've seen here. I want you to say you've been hanging out with Aiden, and you can say he was staying here. He told you the old lady was his granny. That's it. Can you manage that, Georgie boy?"

"Yes, sir."

"Good lad."

Spike handed a few notes over to George, who took them and put them in his pocket.

"Go grab your bike and be on your way, George."

George remained standing for a few seconds longer, seemingly uneasy about leaving.

"Off you go, George," Spike repeated firmly.

George jolted into action, ran over to where his bike was leaning against the lounge wall and made his way to the front door. As he was almost away, a voice called out to him.

"Go easy, George," said young Aiden.

George turned and looked at his friend. He was going to miss him.

"Yeah, good luck, Aiden," he said before turning away and out of the front door, which Spike closed firmly behind him. He was gone.

"So, am I going to Bradford now?" asked Aiden.

"Not a fucking chance. You're going nowhere near Bradford. I just don't want George knowing where you're going." Spike moved closer to Aiden and looked right down at him. "And I'll tell you something else, son. If you try to contact George again, Mr Hazell will have you killed. Have you got that?"

"Yeah, I got it," answered Aiden.

"Good. Right, come on, let's go. We're getting out of here before the pigs arrive. Leave the old dear in her room, she'll soon figure out we've gone. Come on, let's split."

9

DS Fazli Masoud had been working hard, calling in favours, and had managed to obtain a location where the phone number obtained from Joanne's phone had been used a great deal over recent days and weeks. Even though the phone had been shut down, it was still possible to get the location, which was pinpointed to an address on a housing estate on the east side of Harrogate, close to Harrogate hospital, where Rosie and a team of detectives and officers were ready to approach.

"Is that the right flat, Faz?" asked Rosie as she pointed to the council-owned ground floor flat.

"That's definitely the one, boss," replied Masoud, who as well as obtaining the necessary authorisation to carry out the raid, had carried out checks to eliminate nearby flats and properties. "The tenant is a Mrs Margaret Church. She's seventy-seven years old."

Rosie looked around one more time before speaking into the Airwave radio to check that everyone was in place, including officers round the back. The replies confirmed that they were.

"Right, come on then, Faz. Let's go."

Earlier, the gendarmes had been to the address found on Louie's person. The man there, thirty-nine-year-old

Jeremy Knowles, had been uncooperative at first, but was soon persuaded by French and Leblanc to play ball. Once Mr Knowles had been informed of the trouble he could be facing, all attempts to deny any knowledge and protest his innocence were replaced with helpful assistance and some useful information, such as details on how the transactions were arranged and carried out, and by whom. A useful description of one of the young runners had been given, and it turned out that the number he had called for drug supplies was indeed the same as the one Joanne Chapman had been using.

Rosie didn't think any of the criminals would be at the flat, believing that they had vacated the property, but she couldn't take any chances. There was still a chance, however unlikely, that the gang could have been slow to realise they had left clues and take appropriate action, meaning that there could be some nasty people inside. Her next mission would be to ensure that Mrs Church was safe. Then she would order a thorough search of the property while Mrs Church was being questioned.

When Rosie and Masoud approached the front door, she paused to look around one more time before knocking on the door.

There was no answer. Rosie tried again and shouted through the letterbox.

"Hello, Mrs Church. Are you there?"

Again, nothing happened. Rosie tried again.

"Mrs Church. I'm Detective Chief Inspector Rosie Marks, could you please come to the door for me."

She waited a few more seconds before talking into the radio, asking if there had been any activity around the rear.

There hadn't. Rosie's thoughts started to turn towards the possibility of having the door rammed open, but as the tenant was elderly, she felt she should wait a little longer and try again. She bent down to shout into the letterbox one more time, but a voice on the radio interrupted her.

"There's someone at the window, boss," came the voice of an officer watching the rear of the property. "A lady looking right at us. I'm moving over to speak with her."

"Tell her to answer the door."

"I'm trying. It'll be easier if I can get her to open her window."

"Should I come round?" Rosie barked into the radio.

"Wait, boss," came the reply. "She's going, I think she's got the message."

Rosie bent down to the letterbox again, this time peering through to see inside. A few seconds later an old lady appeared. She was dressed in a worn and dirty looking nightie, and was hobbling along a short hallway with the aid of two NHS standard issue silver walking sticks, making her way towards the front door. Rosie could see she didn't look a happy customer.

"What t' bloody hell's all this about?" she barked in a broad Yorkshire accent. She was clearly annoyed. "Finally, I get some peace and quiet, and now I'm being attacked by t' law."

Rosie heard every word and knew for certain that the gangsters had gone.

"Pretty sure Mrs Church is alone," she said into the radio. "But take nothing for granted."

By now Mrs Church had made it to the door and started fiddling with the lock. "What d'ya want?" she shouted.

"Margaret," said Rosie, speaking in a calm manner, trying the friendly approach. "I'm Rosie from the police. We have reason to believe that you've had visitors here lately that we need to speak with you about. Please can you open the door?"

With the warrant they had obtained, Rosie was well within her rights to order a forced entry into the property. However, it would be much better if Mrs Church opened the door and invited them in.

Slowly the door opened a little, and a face appeared in the small gap.

"What is it?" said the old lady.

"Margaret," said Rosie, now with a little more authority. "Right now, is there anyone else in your home?"

"No, they've all cleared off, thank God. And taken all their shit with them."

"Margaret, these people are wanted criminals who we're looking for. We need to come in and ask you some questions about them. Can we come in, please?"

Mrs Church opened the door. "Come on then."

Rosie stood aside and waved in a team of officers to secure the flat. They quickly swarmed the small property and a few seconds later Rosie got the all-clear. Mrs Church was indeed alone.

"Let's go inside, Margaret," said Rosie. "We need to talk, sweetheart."

Glancing around, Rosie noted that the place was untidy and dirty. It was obvious that Mrs Church was struggling with her health, so a certain degree of disorder and grubbiness could be forgiven. However, the fact that a gang had taken over the flat had obviously made things significantly worse. County lines drug gangs weren't known for their cleaning and tidying skills but she'd seen much worse in her experience of visiting the homes of county lines victims, especially the addicts themselves.

"Let's sit down here and have a chat, Margaret," she said pointing to the worn and tatty sofa.

Rosie helped Mrs Church sit down before sitting in an armchair right opposite.

"Okay, Margaret," she said. "I know you've had unwanted guests in your home lately, and I'm so sorry about that. As you probably realised, these people are nasty criminals, and I want to catch them for what they've done to you, and put them away. So, we need to search this property, and I need to get the officers to start now. Do you understand?"

"Yes, I understand."

While the officers searched the property, Rosie, with Masoud sitting in the other armchair, began the interview.

"Margaret, tell me how these criminals first made contact with you."

"Well," said Mrs Church, frowning as her memory kicked in. "I were struggling with my heavy shopping trolley one day, trying to get it in t' front door, when a young man and a teenage boy appeared out of nowhere."

"What did they do?" asked Rosie.

"They wanted to help me."

"And did they help you, Mrs Church?" asked Masoud.

"Oh aye," replied Mrs Church, turning to look at him. "They lifted t' trolley, which were heavy y'know, and even unpacked and put t' shopping away in t' cupboards for me."

"What happened next?" asked Rosie.

"Well, they told me to sit down and put my feet up and made me a cup of tea."

"That sounds like a nice thing to do," said Rosie. "So, then what happened?"

"We got talking about stuff, you know, everyday chat about family and friends, neighbours, did I get lots of visitors, do I go out much, does a doctor or a nurse ever visit."

"And what did you tell them?" asked Rosie.

"I told them I didn't have any family or friends, at least none that bother coming to see me, and that I never hear from t' neighbours. Don't even know their names." Mrs Church paused while she thought back to what had happened. "They were casing me out, weren't they? They just seemed like nice lads to me at t' time."

"They were casing you out, Mrs Church," Rosie confirmed. "They wanted to know if your flat was likely to be a safe place for what they had in mind. And they weren't nice lads, were they?"

"No, they were horrible. But I couldn't do owt to stop 'em. They came back next day and said they needed a place to stay for a while, and so they were stopping here. I said they couldn't stay in this little flat, but they weren't so friendly this time. They said I had no choice."

"So they just moved in?" asked Masoud, shaking his head. Was it really that easy to take over a vulnerable person's home?

"Aye, lad. In they came with loads of stuff. At least they did t' shopping, so I didn't have to leave t' flat, or owt. But they weren't nice boys, they were up to bad things. They had drugs you know."

"I know they did, Mrs Church," said Rosie. "So, has anything happened here this morning?"

"Oh, aye," Mrs Church replied. "There's been more visitors here this morning, just before they all finally buggered off."

"Tell us exactly what happened."

Mrs Church went on to explain that there had been a group of people at her home a couple of hours earlier, but after some harsh talking by an angry sounding man, they had all left. Rosie was particularly interested in the old lady's account of how one young lad had been forced to wait with her in the bedroom for a while before being summoned. Although the boy appeared to be scared, he had, according to Mrs Church, been pushing his ear to the wall in an effort to listen to what had been going on in the lounge. Rosie asked Mrs Church to describe the boy, and what she said gave Rosie the impression it could have been George Potter.

"Let me show you something, Mrs Church," said Rosie as she retrieved her phone and started scrolling through photographs. She had remembered that some months before, Helen Potter had sent her some family pictures. When she found the one she was looking for, she held it

68

up so Mrs Church could see it. "Is this the lad who was with you in your bedroom this morning?"

"Oh aye, that's him. Nice young kid. I've seen him here a few times recently."

So, thought Rosie, young George has been here a few times, and he wasn't at school this morning as his mother had assumed. Helen really had taken her eye off the ball as far as George was concerned. Rosie needed to find George as soon as possible. As well as trying to help her friend's son, she had some important questions for him.

When the search was over and Rosie had finished with Mrs Church, everything of potential interest was taken away and Rosie explained what would happen next. The old lady seemed to be in good spirits, considering what she'd been going through, and the medic that Rosie had summoned to the scene was satisfied that she was in good shape.

With everything completed and in order, Rosie and the officers left and headed back to the station.

10

Forty-year-old Camilla Bryant sat alone in her flat in Blackburn, Lancashire. Photographs of her young son were hanging on the walls around her, with more propped up on a sideboard and the mantlepiece.

She took a sip from a mug of hot coffee, then picked up a half-finished cigarette from an overfilled ashtray and took a long, greedy drag from it. She was a shadow of her former self; the confident, assured and capable single mother she had been up until only a few weeks ago.

Camilla had been through hell and was sick with worry. *Why had Louie gone? He'd been happy at home, hadn't he? Where had he gone? Who was Louie with? Was he even alive? If so, why didn't he just call to say he's okay? Is it my fault? It must be my fault. I'm a horrible, pathetic mother. I let him down. I should have been there for him.*

As she ran a hand through her short Afro hair, tears flowed down her cheeks. Yet again. As Camilla reached for another smoke, she was rudely interrupted by a loud knock at the door. She froze. Was this the call she had been dreading?

She stood up and made her way out of her lounge into the hall, and turned to face the front door. Through the opaque glass, Camilla could see what was without doubt the figures of two uniformed police officers.

"Oh my god," she squealed.

"Mrs Bryant," shouted one of the officers, making Camilla jump. "Are you in?"

Camilla made her way to the door and slowly opened it wide. She stood back, mouth wide open, eyes like saucers, as she focused on the two policewomen stood before her. She knew what this meant.

"Hello, Mrs Bryant," said one of the officers. "I'm PC Nahla Ahmed, this is PC Sue Bellingham. We need to speak to you about your son, Louie."

"Oh my god!" Camilla screamed. "It's bad news, isn't it?"

"Please calm down, Mrs Bryant," said the constable. "It's not the worst news, Louie is alive but is poorly. Let's go in so we can explain."

"What?" said Camilla, still rooted to the spot, leaving the officers out in the cold rain. "He's alive?"

"Yes, he's alive," said PC Bellingham. "Let's go inside, shall we?"

"Oh, okay," whispered Camilla. She stood back to allow the officers through, closed the door and followed them into the lounge.

"That's better," said PC Ahmed. "Would you like to sit down?"

"No," Camilla answered. "Just tell me what's happened."

"I'm afraid Louie was stabbed yesterday evening and is in a critical condition in hospital."

"Oh my god," squealed Camilla, not for the first time. "How bad it is?"

"It's serious, but he's in good hands and we're hopeful of a full recovery."

"Okay. I need to see him. Now! The hospital's not far. I'll go straight away."

"It's not that simple, Mrs Bryant," said PC Ahmed. "Louie is in hospital in Harrogate."

"Harrogate? What's he doing there?"

"We don't know yet. The police over there are looking into that. He may have been there since he went missing, maybe not. We don't know. The important thing is that we bring you up to date."

"How can I get to Harrogate?"

"I suggest you get someone to drive you there, a friend perhaps, or a family member. Or you could get a train across. I don't know the route, but I would think you'd need to go to Leeds then transfer to Harrogate."

"I'll get the train. This afternoon. Now."

"Okay. I'll let the officers over in Harrogate know so they can expect you. Can I take your phone number? You might get a call from an officer over there to make arrangements for you to see Louie."

"Okay. Thank you."

PC Ahmed took a note of Camilla's phone number before speaking to her again.

"Is there anything else we can do for you, Mrs Bryant?"

"I don't think so. Thank you for coming."

"You're welcome. We'll see ourselves out."

Camilla sat down and lit another cigarette. It was good news, it had to be. Louie was alive. She looked in her purse and counted the money. It wasn't enough, so she went to a cupboard to get an envelope of cash she'd been keeping for Louie. She had put away as much as she could, thinking that when Louie finally did turn up, or call, she would have something to help him with, or maybe to tempt him back, to buy him something special to heal their relationship.

She grabbed a fistful of notes and shoved them into her purse then headed into the bedroom where she changed into outdoor clothes and stuffed some spare clothing into a backpack. She then found an overcoat, slipped into her shoes, grabbed an umbrella, and headed out.

Camilla Bryant was going to see her son.

***

Louie Bryant had undergone life-saving surgery as soon as he'd arrived at the hospital the evening before. The operation had been complicated, but after hours in theatre in the good hands of an experienced surgeon, Louie's prospects were looking far more positive.

However, there was still a long way to go. Louie was being looked after and monitored by nurses, with regular visits by a doctor to make sure his recovery was going to plan.

During the morning, he'd opened his eyes a few times, but had soon drifted off again. At around midday, he'd managed to look around a little more, taking note of his surroundings. A nurse had asked him if he was okay, and gently explained that he had been injured but was on the mend. He was told to rest and let the healing take its time. He seemed to accept the advice and relaxed before drifting back to sleep for a while.

However, early in the afternoon, Louie fully woke up in a startled state and began shouting.

"Calm down, Louie," said a nurse who had appeared straight away. "You're okay now, just relax and you'll soon get better."

Louie shouted again, something about his mother and wanting to go home. The nurse called for a doctor before trying to calm the young patient once again.

"Relax, Louie," she gently said while using a small towel to wipe the sweat off his forehead. "We're expecting your mother to come soon to visit you."

It wasn't working, as Louie kept yelling. He needed help, shouting that there was blood everywhere. He then began to get even more agitated while saying that he hated Freddy and wouldn't do his shitty work for him anymore.

The doctor appeared and sedated him once again, which did the trick as Louie fell asleep.

"That'll keep him quiet for a while," said the doctor. "He's gone through a terrible ordeal and is bound to be traumatised. Keep an eye on him, sister. I'll be back in an hour or so to see how he's doing."

"Yes, doctor," the nurse replied.

All of this was overheard by the officer on duty outside the ward, and was soon reported back to the station.

It was going to be a while before the doctors would allow Louie to be questioned by the police, but Rosie made a mental note to make sure she was the first to talk to him, as soon as that was possible.

Rosie also wanted to speak with Louie's mother, Camilla Bryant, whom she had discovered was on her way to Harrogate by train to see her son. Rosie decided she would meet Camilla at the station and take her to the hospital herself.

11

Spike inserted a key into the front door of a flat occupied by an elderly gentleman, turned it, entered, and looked around. Bill Hathaway, a frail and vulnerable old man, who was suffering from Parkinson's disease, sat in his armchair staring up at the thug in shock.

"This'll do nicely, Bill," Spike announced as he continued his survey of the premises. "At least for now."

"Who are you, son?" Bill asked.

"I'm your new guest, Billy boy. Everyone calls me Spike."

Before the arrival of Spike in Harrogate, Hazell's trusted enforcer, Mark Thompson, known by the street name Tommy, had instructed the local handler Freddy to find a new location to move into and operate from for a while.

It had been an easy assignment for Freddy as he'd already discovered an ideal place and done the groundwork to ensure that it would be safe to use. Bill Hathaway had been easy to manipulate, and it would be an ideal location to use as a trap house for a while, as long as they weren't there too long.

"Some lad came here recently," said Bill, his whole body shaking more than usual. "He said someone would arrive soon. He even took a front door key with him. Said I had no choice in the matter."

"Yeah, that's right. That was Freddy, and this is the front door key." Spike waved the key at Bill, looking down on him with contempt. "I'll be using this for a while, Billy boy."

"So, tell me again, son. What are you doing in my house?" Bill asked.

"This is where I'll be hanging out for a while, Bill," Spike replied as he removed his dark, decorated hoodie and threw it over the back of the sofa.

Bill looked down and noticed the large image stitched onto one side; a bony fist with the middle finger sticking up in a rude gesture. Charming, he thought.

"What's wrong with somewhere else then, son? Plenty of hotels around here, you know."

Spike turned back to Bill, an evil sneer on his face. He wasn't someone many would pick a fight with, certainly not an old, sick man like Bill. He stood at around six feet tall, was well-built and clearly powerful. His head was shaved, highlighting an assortment of tattoos.

"I don't need no fucking hotel, Billy boy," he shouted, making Bill jump back, and nearly fall over in the process; he grabbed the back of a nearby armchair for support. "You and your gaff have been selected, old fella, so it's your privilege to enjoy my company."

"Oh," said Bill, starting to finally accept that he had no choice in the matter. "Right you are, son."

"And let me explain a few other things to you, Billy, old son. A few ground rules. Number one, you're gonna spend most of your time in this lounge, out of my fucking way.

You can sleep in here, as I'll be using your room for myself for a while. You got that?"

Bill stood in silence watching Spike, his whole body shaking once again, and not just due to his illness. Spike was a scary young man, and Bill was frightened.

Spike shouted, making Bill jump once again. "I said, do you fucking understand?"

"Yes, okay. I understand. Where am I supposed to sleep?"

"On the fucking sofa, of course. While I'm gone you can move your gear in here, can't you? I just need you outta my way."

"Yes, okay."

"Good, we're getting somewhere. Rule number two; you don't say a word to anyone, and I mean anyone, about me being here, or anything about what you might see going on here. That clear?"

"Crystal clear."

"What family have you got, Billy? You got any kids?"

"I haven't got any kids."

"Yeah, that's what I heard. What about friends? Who do you hang out with?"

"I don't have any friends anymore, not since I've been ill and housebound."

"That's what I heard too. That's why you were selected, old man."

"I know a few people down at my allotment, but I haven't heard from them for a while."

"What about neighbours? Got any nosy ones?"

"We all keep ourselves to ourselves round here."

"That's what I wanna hear, Billy boy. So, I just need to explain one more thing to you." Spike came closer to Bill once again, leaning down so his forehead rested on Bill's. Looking right into the old man's eyes, he spoke slowly with clear emphasis. "What I want you to be clear about is that if you tell anyone about me, anyone at all, I *will* kill you."

Bill didn't dare move, as he took in the words, knowing he was in a bad situation and there was absolutely nothing he could do about it.

"What did I just say to you, Billy boy?"

Bill was frozen in fear, the only movement coming from the uncontrollable shaking from his head right down to his toes. A few seconds went by before Spike shouted once again.

"What the fuck did I just explain to you, old man?"

Although nearly paralysed, Bill started to stutter a response. "If, if I, tell anyone, about you, about you being here, you're gonna, kill me."

"Now we're getting somewhere. And do you think I'll keep my promise about that, Billy?"

Bill was petrified. He knew, without any doubt, that the man was indeed easily capable of taking someone's life, and believed that, in fact, he had already done so, more than likely on numerous occasions, and knew that if he stepped out of line Spike would indeed kill him.

"Well?" Spike bellowed, still pushing his forehead down on Bill's.

"Yes, Spike, I believe you."

"Good," said Spike, moving away and walking towards the door to the kitchen. Bill found himself staring at a tattoo of a swastika etched on the left side of Spike's head, just behind his ear. As Spike peered into the small kitchen, Bill saw a tattoo of a religious cross on the back of his neck, and then another of an ugly, rather deadly looking spider behind his right ear.

"This kitchen's a bit fucking poky, Billy boy. It'll have to do, I suppose."

Bill just stood, still holding onto the armchair for support, wondering how his life had changed for the worse so suddenly. Spike came back and spoke to him.

"I need to go and get some gear organised, so I'll be gone for a while; back later tonight. When I get back, I'll be bringing gear inside so I can start work. So, old man, just so we're clear, when I get back, I'll be using the bedroom. And most important of all, if I find that you've done something stupid, like tell anyone about me, if I see any nasty surprises, or any shit like that, you know what I'll do to you, right, Billy boy?"

"I get the picture, son," said Bill.

"Good. Then I'll be on my way. See you later, try not to miss me too much."

12

Brian Hazell was sitting in the front of his swanky Mercedes limousine on the journey west, away from Harrogate and heading towards Blackburn. There was a deathly silence in the car, so he turned to Freddy and said, "What's up, Freddy? Cat got your tongue, lad?"

Freddy shrugged his shoulders. He was clearly not happy about being moved on.

"Listen, Freddy," Hazell said to him. "I couldn't let you stay back there. What if that boy, the copper's son, starts talking and can identify you?"

"He can identify Spike," Freddy pointed out.

"That he can, but Spike has a certain, what's the word, aura about him. That kid'll be too scared to ID Spike. Anyway, you'll do great in Blackburn. Tell you what, give it a month and I'll get you down to my club for a night of fun, yeah?"

Freddy raised his head and saw the smile on Hazell's face.

"Does that sound like a plan, Freddy boy?" added Hazell.

"Are you serious?" asked Freddy, his eyes now lit up. The thought of an invite to Hazell's club for a night had picked him up.

"Course I'm serious, lad. After a month, provided you're getting results, speak with Tommy and we'll get it organised."

"Okay, boss. Thanks."

"No problem," said Hazell as his eyes shifted over to where young Jamie was sitting. He wondered what he should say to him, but his thoughts were interrupted as his phone buzzed. He took it out of his pocket; it was the message he'd been waiting for. He read it through and saw to his joy that his source at Greater Manchester police had suggested three possibilities at Harrogate police station. Alongside each one was the reason for his belief that they could be ripe for an offer of some kind, and he'd very kindly sent their telephone numbers.

Hazell read the message through once again before composing a reply.

> **This is bloody useful! Good job.**
> **There'll be a bonus waiting for you**
> **when you come to see Anya. I'll be**
> **in touch if I need anything else!**

Hazell read the message through again, hit the send button and replaced the phone in his pocket. Then, as they passed over the rocky hills of the southern tip of the Yorkshire Dales, he contemplated who at Harrogate police station he would approach with an offer.

It would have to be good. An *incentive* they would find impossible to ignore, and extremely hard to refuse.

After a few minutes thinking it through, it became clear to Hazell who he should target. An officer who had a compelling reason to seek something he could provide, in abundance.

Hazell then composed another text message, this time on a different burner phone he kept for high-risk occasions. If it went wrong, he would quickly dispose of it. Without mentioning his own name, and carefully choosing his words to tempt the recipient into taking a huge plunge, Hazell wrote his message.

After reading it through a couple of times, he hit the send button.

He was fishing. If, by some chance, he got the bite he was looking for, he may very well get himself a special prize. An informer on the inside of Harrogate police station.

Hazell took one more quick glance over his shoulder. Freddy was smiling again, but Jamie still looked miserable. Eye contact was made for half a second before Jamie looked away. Hazell returned to looking at his phone.

***

Jamie looked out of the side window, but was oblivious to the stunning countryside views. He had just made momentary eye contact with the boss, but had been too scared to talk to him, so looked away. A conversation was the last thing he wanted, but he was itching to know what was going to happen to him when they reached their destination, wherever that destination was.

Jamie knew he had messed up his assignment. This was to have been his first kill, having been coerced into carrying it out by both Freddy and Tommy, who had been on the phone beforehand, reminding him of why it was important for him to carry out the mission. Apart from the promised rewards, which Jamie had started to believe would never be realised, there were the ever-present threats to his family. Any fuckups, and there would be repercussions, Tommy had said. And he believed him.

He noticed Hazell looking round at him again, but this time Jamie forced himself to hold his stare. He was petrified, scared for his life, and for the lives and safety of his family. Somehow, and from somewhere, Jamie found the courage to speak.

"M-Mr Hazell," he began. "Where are you taking me?"

"We're taking you back for more training, lad," Hazell replied, his eyes piercing right into the young man's soul. "We're gonna knock you into shape."

"Oh, okay."

"You up for that, Jamie boy?"

"Yes, sir," said Jamie, slightly relieved, but not altogether convinced. "And when can I see my family?"

"I don't know about that, son. Let's see how you get on back at HQ."

"Oh, okay. Thanks."

Hazell looked down at his phone once again, and Jamie returned to his thoughts. He'd been wondering how his failure to kill Louie would affect his family, the family he had willingly run away from, having been persuaded that a better, vastly more exciting and lucrative life awaited by joining the gang. He recalled what they had told him to persuade him to get away, leaving no trace of his whereabouts. Who needs a shitty family? Who needs school? Who needs a job, when you can make big money coming with us? And the women? Who doesn't want a good, regular shag with a real lady any time they want? A woman who knows how to really please a man like you.

However, once he'd been moved away, many miles from home, the doubts had set in. Of course, there were no women, not for a lowly runner like him, but the real issue was the horror of the awful things he was being asked to do, along with the regular beatings he had to endure, as they knocked him into shape, supposedly for his own good. Or, just for daring to question things, or to even think about leaving. The beatings were brutal. Then, the threats to his family had begun.

When Freddy and Tommy, along with the fearsome Whacko, told him what would happen to his mum and dad if he stepped out of line, he realised he had no choice but to comply. And worse still, they explained what they were going to do to his little sister unless he accepted all future assignments and carried them out to their complete satisfaction. He believed them, every word they said.

"Tell you what, Jamie boy," said Hazell, interrupting his thoughts and making him jump. "If you can sort your shit out, and actually do what we need you to do, you'll be back in favour again. Know what I mean?"

"Er, yes, sir."

"You too can come down to my club and enjoy yourself for a few hours, just like Freddy's gonna do. Sample some of the products, have a few beers, let yourself go with a lady of your fancy. Ain't that right, Freddy?"

"You betcha, boss."

"You fancy some of that kind of action, kiddo?"

"Yes, sir."

"Then get your finger out your arse and start doing what you're told, son."

As Hazell returned his attention to his phone, a tear rolled down Jamie's face as he contemplated his situation. He'd been trained to carry out various missions involving the delivery of drugs, which were easy enough to do. But when it was explained to him that they wanted to train him up for something much more important, that he'd been selected for special assignments, he had dreaded what was in store for him. To his horror, they wanted him to terminate those selected for execution, and they started to train him to do so.

They wanted him to be an assassin.

A killer.

So, now Brian Hazell was telling him that if he did his job properly, he would be rewarded. *Go and kill whoever we want assassinated, and we'll see you get to have a good time.* Well, he didn't believe it. He knew he was being lied to, because he'd heard it all before. But, because of the threats to his family, he had no choice but to comply. At least it looked like he wasn't going to be killed for his failure, which was a positive.

Jamie noticed that they had arrived in Blackburn. The car pulled into a layby on a quiet road on a housing estate, and Hazell got out. He walked around the car and opened the door for Freddy, who also got out. As Jamie watched the two of them talking, he carefully tried to open the door next to him. If it opened, he'd unclip his seatbelt, make a break for it, and head for home. He was a good runner, and would easily lose anyone chasing him. He silently groaned as the handle pulled all the way back, but the door remained closed. The child lock had been activated: he was trapped.

When Hazell had finished speaking with Freddy, he got back in the car and they drove away. Jamie looked back and watched Freddy walk away in the icy rain, huddled up under his hoodie, marching towards wherever he had been ordered to go. Jamie was envious, wishing he too could be free to walk away.

After a short while, Jamie saw a road sign indicating they were heading towards Bolton. He discerned therefore that they were going in the general direction of Manchester, which he took to be a good sign.

Once again, Hazell turned around to look at him. They locked eyes for short while, and Hazell winked at him before returning to his phone. Jamie's thoughts then turned to the mission he had been tasked to carry out the day before. He had to kill the enemy; the young lad called Louie. The young man who had been in the same boat as him, caught in the snare of evil gangsters, just wanting to get out and go home. He had been shown how to use a knife, how to twist it to cause maximum damage. The evil monster, known as Whacko, had hammered home his point, saying "This is how a knife will carve up the insides of your little sister, Jamie boy. Right after I've fucked her, over and over, while she screamed for mercy". That thought, along with the image of that brutal thug even touching his innocent sister, let alone abusing and killing her, had been more than enough to persuade him to comply.

But he had failed. He was too scared to take his time to do it properly, or maybe he just didn't want to succeed.

Maybe he couldn't kill another poor kid caught up in the same mess he had been subjected to, even though he had to. And to make his situation worse, he had completely forgotten to empty the boy's pockets as instructed.

Jamie was wondering how he would ever manage to kill anyone. He was in an impossible situation: either kill, or they would harm or even kill his family, or kill him! He knew he had to go along with it, at least until he could find a way to escape and get back to his family, maybe get the police involved.

He snapped out of his thoughts as he realised that they had turned off a main road and were heading up a track. It looked and felt more like a bridle path than a road. They were in an isolated and lonely place in the countryside, with no one else in sight. Again, he wanted to ask where they were going, but didn't dare. Something wasn't right, and a sudden dread overtook him. His stomach tightened as nerves kicked in: he was in the grip of fear.

They turned a corner on the gravelly surface and came to a halt next to another car. He noticed a dinghy tied onto a roof rack. The front doors opened, and two figures got out. Squinting through the rain covered window, he saw two men. The first large man had familiar multicoloured hair, the other huge man, with no hair at all, possessed the most evil face Jamie had ever seen. He knew who they were. The two men moving towards Jamie were Tommy and Whacko.

Jamie's heart skipped a beat. This didn't look at all good. He looked around at Hazell who had turned to face him with a nasty, evil grin on his face.

"This is where you get off, Jamie lad."

"Wait a minute," squealed Jamie. "What do you mean? You said I was going for more training."

"I lied. This is the end of the line for you, son. I won't have failures in my organisation, you must have noticed that."

"But, Mr Hazell, sir. Please give me another chance. I know I didn't do a good job, but it was my first time, and it won't happen again."

Hazell didn't reply. He just kept the evil, twisted smirk on his face as the two men on the outside moved around the limousine. The door flew open, and Jamie felt a strong hand reach across, unclip the seatbelt, grab his arm and drag him out of the car. Jamie nearly flew out of the motor, such was the force used, and found himself in a heap on the wet, cold ground.

"Hello, once again, young Jamie," said the voice of the evil Whacko. "I was just on my way to pay a visit to your kid sister, as it happens, when Mr Hazell called and asked me to come and see you."

"Please don't!" shouted Jamie, helpless and powerless to do anything to help himself. "Mr Hazell. Please give me another chance, I won't let you down."

Whacko pulled him up, grabbed the front of his hoodie and pulled his face into his own. Jamie was shocked by the pure evil in the brutal thug's piercing grey eyes. His ugly, wicked smirk remained, while his nostrils were flared in apparent excitement. This monster was welcoming the obvious sadistic pleasure he was about to savour. His breath stank, a noxious mixture of warm nicotine and halitosis, which rushed down into Jamie's lungs, causing nausea and dizziness. His stomach churned with bile, and all feeling had disappeared from his legs. As fear completely took over, Jamie lost all control of his bowels and bladder, and was painfully aware that he was urinating and defecating into his underpants. To complete his utter shame and humiliation, excrement began soaking through his light-blue jeans.

"Fuck me," shouted Tommy, laughing while pointing at Jamie. "He's shat himself!"

"You're a dirty little fucker," sneered Whacko, who with enormous power, grabbed Jamie's shoulders and twisted him around so he faced the limo once again. He looked and saw Hazell standing alongside Tommy. They were both laughing, mocking him as he struggled to remain upright, all hope of a happy way out of this pain and misery finally gone. How did I ever get mixed up with these animals, he asked himself.

"Mr Hazell, ple—"

Jamie's words were broken off as Whacko violently twisted his head with such force that a gut-churning snap rang out as the sleet and icy rain descended around them.

Jamie hadn't heard anything. By the time the sound of his neck being broken reached his ears and was on its way to being processed by his brain, he was dead.

His lifeless body slumped to the ground in a heap.

***

"Right, good job, Whack," said Hazell. "You know what to do, guys."

"Yes, boss," said Tommy. "Usual place, usual method. Everything's set up, we're clear to go. We'll get rid of him later tonight. I'll call you when it's done."

As Hazell was driven away, Tommy and Whacko loaded the corpse into a body bag and dropped him into the boot of their motor.

The men had a special place for the unwanted bodies of their victims, and Jamie was to be taken there and dumped. The chances of him ever being discovered were negligible.

13

Just as it was starting to get dark, Rosie was waiting in the main foyer of Harrogate railway station, holding a large piece of card in front of her. The name written on the front, scribbled using a large felt tip pen, was CAMILLA BRYANT.

The train from Leeds had just arrived, and commuters were making their way from the platform, through the turnstiles and into the station before heading out into the car park or onto Station Parade. It was a busy time of day.

An attractive lady, with dark skin, soft brown eyes and a friendly smile, approached Rosie and spoke.

"Hello, Rosie. I'm Camilla."

"Hello, Camilla," said Rosie as she folded up the card and placed it in a nearby bin. "I didn't see you among the crowd. Welcome to Harrogate. Let's go and see Louie."

"Yes please."

Rosie led Camilla outside and into her car and drove the short distance to the hospital.

Within fifteen minutes, they had parked and were walking along various hospital corridors to the ward where Louie was being treated. The police officer guarding the patient recognised Rosie approaching and stood up to let her inside the room, though Rosie still presented her ID as she passed, escorting Camilla into the ward, and taking care to keep a gentle hand on her arm just in case she felt the urge to jump forward to embrace her son.

She needn't have worried. Camilla just stood next to the bed, hand over her mouth, gazing down at Louie, who was asleep.

"Camilla," said Rosie quietly. "So we're all sure, can you confirm to me that this is Louie?"

"Oh, yes," she replied, tears starting to fall once again. "This is Louie. Oh my god, how did this happen to you?"

"Why don't you sit down, sweetheart," said Rosie as she pulled a chair over to the side of the bed. "Then I'll get you a cup of tea, or coffee if you prefer."

"Oh, thank you," Camilla replied as she sat down. "I could murder a cup of coffee."

"We don't like using the 'M' word around here, but I'll organise a drink for you. How do you like your coffee?"

"Oh, yeah, sorry. Er, white with no sugar, please."

Rosie left Camilla in the ward holding Louie's hand as she went to get her drink. When she returned a few minutes later, Camilla was excited. It seemed that Louie was waking up once again. How's that for timing, Rosie thought.

Sure enough, Louie's eyes started to open. It took a while, but when he'd clearly woken up, he looked around the room and reminding himself where he was and why he was there. Just before the panic set in once again as the nearby nurse had feared, his gaze fell upon the smiling face of his mother. He paused a few seconds, just staring at her, before tears started to fall.

"Oh, darling," said Camilla, still holding his hand. "I've missed you so much."

"I wanted so much to come home, Mum," said Louie as the tears flowed. "They wouldn't let me, so they tried to kill me."

"Hello, Louie," said Rosie, interrupting the precious moment, but fully aware of the power of a dying declaration. She wasn't expecting Louie to die at that moment, but one never knew what was around the corner. "I'm Rosie, from the local police. Do you know who tried to kill you?"

Louie took a few deep breaths, as if summoning up the power to speak.

"It was Jamie. I don't know his surname, but I saw him a few times before."

"Okay, sweetheart. Thank you. I'll have more questions sometime soon, but I'll leave you to talk with your mother."

"I was coming home, Mum. But they stopped me."

"Oh, darling," cried Camilla. "I've been so worried. Soon as you're better you can come home, and we can start again. Everything will be fine, I promise."

Rosie had taken a seat in the corner of the room, keeping out of the way for a while, although still keen to hear every word. After twenty minutes or so of Louie speaking with his mother while drifting in and out of sleep, the nurse announced that enough was enough. They had to leave.

Camilla had called while en route to the hospital and booked a room at a local Premier Inn, so Rosie drove her there. Camilla would be back in the morning to see Louie.

Rosie had somewhere else to go before driving home. She was desperate to speak to George Potter. His mother had confirmed that he was home, so Rosie headed off to the Potter household for what would hopefully be a useful conversation with George.

14

Rosie took a long sip of coffee, savoured the taste, and placed the mug down on the fancy looking dining room table, taking care to make sure it was in the middle of the coaster. She didn't want to mark the solid oak tabletop.

As she waited for Helen to fetch George, she looked around. The open plan dining room and lounge had comfortable furniture and was well decorated. Family photos were placed around the room and hung on walls, alongside a painting showing a countryside scene. Rosie wasn't much of an art lover, so the painting didn't do much for her but she did take a good look at the photos of smiling faces, showing a happy, close family.

Movement caught her eye. She turned and saw a young face at the doorway. The gaunt, pale, yet despite all, smiling young Jack looked back at her.

"Hello, Jack," said Rosie smiling back. "Come here and give me a cuddle."

Jack ran over and jumped into Rosie's arms. It had been a while since Rosie had seen him.

"Oh, my darling," she said, squeezing as hard as she dared. "Am I glad to see you."

Helen walked into the room, accompanied by a miserable looking George who slumped into a chair at the table. Rosie let Jack go, and his father Gavin took him out of the room.

"See you soon, Jack," said Rosie as he was led away waving back at her.

Helen sat down at the table. "So, Rosie. Before you say anything to George, let me explain a couple of things. You're right, George wasn't at school today, and it turns out he hasn't been there for over a week. I'm fuming that the school didn't contact me about this, and I'll call in the morning for an explanation. But I'm also annoyed that George has been both missing school and hanging out with apparent criminals. However, I've explained to him that whatever's happened, we are here for him, and we will get through this, whatever it takes. That means no matter what he's been involved with, we will do what we have to do to work it out."

Rosie paused to make sure Helen had finished before speaking.

"Okay, Helen," she began. "I completely agree that everything can be worked out, and of course I'm here to help in any way I can with that."

"Thank you, Rosie," said Helen.

Rosie looked over to where George was sitting. Although he was staring down at the tabletop, she began talking to him.

"George, please understand that I'm talking to you this evening as a friend more than a police officer, although as you're a key witness we will have to do things properly, as I'm sure your mother's explained. But before we go through all the formalities, I just want to hear what you have to say so I can get a clearer picture of what's been going on. Is that okay?"

"Yeah, I suppose," replied George, clearly not happy to be there.

"You also need to be aware that I have learned a great deal today about what's been happening, so I probably know a lot more than you realise. There's no point hiding anything from me, especially as I'm here to help you. Do you want my help, George?"

"Dunno. Do I need help?"

"Yes, sweetheart, I think you do. Let me explain it this way. A young man was stabbed yesterday evening and is still fighting for his life in hospital. You know about this, because I saw you at the scene last night. But having put things together, I now know that you weren't at that scene by coincidence, were you? You've been in the company of those who carried out that knife attack, and those who ordered it to happen, and that, by the way, is attempted murder. And if that lad in hospital doesn't make it, it'll be murder. And you're involved. Do you understand?"

George had stopped looking down at the wooden table and was staring into Rosie's eyes. She had his attention.

"And I also happen to know that you were at the home of Mrs Church this morning where a meeting took place. Is that right?"

"But I wasn't at the meeting, honest." George was beginning to see the gravity of the situation he was in.

"I know that, George. You were in the bedroom with Mrs Church while that meeting took place. Am I right?"

"Yes," George whispered, his eyes back on the tabletop.

"Although, I gather you were trying your best to listen to what was being said, yeah?"

"I tried to listen, yes."

"Did you hear anything?"

"Not really," he replied, once again looking at Rosie. "There was a man I don't know. I couldn't see him and I didn't know his voice. He shouted sometimes, but the rest I couldn't hear. He was talking to Aiden about something, then he was telling someone off for, well, he said he had, er, fucked up."

"Oh, George!" said Helen, disgusted that her son had used such language, and had been in the company of those who did.

"It's okay, George," said Rosie reassuringly. "I want you to tell me exactly what you know. Don't be shy about the details. Who was the person the man was telling off?"

"I don't know. I didn't see him. I was told to get in the bedroom before he arrived."

"Was it the person that did the stabbing?"

"I think so, yes."

"Did you ever meet the person who did the stabbing?"

"I don't know, maybe. I might have seen him with Freddy and Aiden."

"Who's Freddy?"

"He's in charge. Well, he was until today."

"What do you mean?"

"Freddy had to go somewhere else, I think I heard the man say he was going to Blackburn. Another man is in charge in Harrogate now."

"Does that person have a name?"

"Yes. His name is Spike."

"Spike? Okay, so did Spike speak with you?"

"Yes. After the man left, Spike got me out of the bedroom and told me to go and never come back."

"Did he, indeed? That's interesting. Did he threaten you? Did he tell you what would happen if you do get in touch again?"

"Not really. He just said that cos Mum's a copper they can't have me there anymore."

"I see. And you're sure you didn't get a look at the man who came to the house?"

"No, I didn't see him at all."

"Okay, George, you're doing great. So, when Spike took you out of the bedroom and into the lounge, who was there?"

"Me, Spike and Aiden."

"Oh yes, I remember Aiden. He was with you last night. We checked the address he gave me, and it was false. He lied to me, didn't he?"

"Yeah, he doesn't come from Harrogate."

"Where does he come from?"

"Blackpool."

Rosie made a note, intending to contact colleagues in Blackpool to see if they knew of an Aiden Gallagher. A thought occurred to her.

"Is his name really Aiden Gallagher?"

"I think so, yeah."

"Okay. So, Spike told you to go home, right?"

"That's right."

"Okay. Do you know where Spike and Aiden went?"

"No, I don't. Although, Spike told me Aiden was going to Bradford to work."

"And you came straight home, is that right?" asked Rosie, again writing the new information down.

"Yes, I came straight home."

The questions and answers continued for another half an hour or so, Rosie being careful to be gentle, all the while taking notes. She was getting a clearer picture of what George knew about the activities of the gang, and what he didn't, and had managed to obtain an initial description of Spike. She was sure that George had not been too deeply involved in what was going on, which was a good thing, and probably why their reaction to the discovery that he was the son of a police officer was simply to insist he went back home and didn't come back. She shuddered at the thought of what might have happened if he had got more involved and knew details about the gang's activities and who the players were. However, something still niggled her. She had to ask something more.

"George," she said. "Tell me, did you ever deliver drugs to people?"

George paused a second before replying.

"No, I didn't."

"Are you sure about that, George?"

"I never took drugs to anyone," he insisted.

"How about Aiden? Did he deliver drugs?"

"Yes, he did. Every day."

"I see. And have you accepted any money from the people you were with?"

Again, George paused, this time for longer.

"Yes, I was given money," he eventually said.

"What did you do with the money?"

"I bought stuff," he said.

Rosie wasn't sure about whether to believe George hadn't been delivering drugs; her instinct was saying that he wasn't telling her everything about his experiences with this gang. However, so far, she had gained some really useful information, and she would be asking more questions the next day in more formal surroundings at the station.

Rosie decided she had done enough, so said her thanks and goodbyes and left. After another, much appreciated hug from Jack, she made her way home.

***

Rosie's phone pinged. She pulled over to read the message.

Hello! Fancy a bevvy?

Rosie's heart skipped a beat. She had recently begun an intimate relationship with DCI Vernon Green, an officer based in the Fulford Road police station in the city of York. After a long time searching for love, she was beginning to believe it had finally arrived. It was still early days, but she felt herself falling for the good-looking, suave Vernon Green. No one else knew about it, but Rosie was starting to think about when she was going to allow their affair to become common knowledge, and most importantly, when and how she was going to introduce him to Sophie.

A bevvy was a code they were using for the short term. Green wasn't enquiring about Rosie's availably to go for a drink, he was suggesting they meet to make love. Rosie had been to his fancy apartment in Harrogate's Montpellier quarter many times over recent weeks and months, and although she was still getting to know more about the man, she was becoming more and more convinced that this time, it was the real thing.

"I'd love a bevvy," she said to herself. "But I have to get home to Sophie."

Rosie composed a reply and hit the send button.

> **I'd love one, darling, but I haven't been home yet. I need to get back home to Sophie. Maybe tomorrow?**

Rosie sighed in disappointment as she waited for the reply. It didn't take long.

> **I'm away tomorrow – will text Saturday when I'm back. xxx**

Rosie put the phone down, restarted her car and headed home.

15

Spike had spent the time since leaving Hathaway's flat journeying over to Blackburn to collect his effects. Having stolen a car, he had collected his things and driven back to Harrogate, and taken them into Bill Hathaway's flat. It was getting late, and he smiled when he saw that Hathaway was fast asleep on the settee. He'd wondered if he would have to grab the pathetic old man and drag him from his bedroom, but Hathaway had obviously listened carefully and had obediently moved into the lounge.

"You alright, Billy boy?" he shouted while switching the bright lounge lights on.

Hathaway jumped out of his sleep, blinking at the light, trying to understand what was happening. Spike moved closer and leant down.

"I say," shouted Spike even louder. "You okay? Did you miss me?"

"Oh, it's you, Spike," said Hathaway, clearly disappointed to see that Spike had returned. He was shaking badly once again.

"Yeah, it's me, old fella. Well don't let me keep you awake, you get some sleep."

Spike laughed as he carried his gear to the bedroom. He hadn't brought much with him; enough gear to get started, and an assortment of clothing. One thing that worried him was an old metal box, the size of a small briefcase, that he carried with him. The box was of particular importance, as it carried the stash of cash and drugs that he had been carefully syphoning off from the business. Back at Blackburn, he had a safe place for it, but now in Harrogate, he didn't have anywhere, so he needed to find one as soon as possible. If Tommy or Whacko were to arrive unannounced and took a look around and found his box, life wouldn't be worth living. In fact, a quick death might be preferable to the fate he would certainly face if he was caught cheating the boss.

Among the things left behind by Freddy, was a list of phone numbers of some of the regular customers, all of whom would need to be informed of the new number to call for supplies. Freddy had helpfully pointed out those who should be contacted first, along with information about them which might prove useful. The number that Spike was looking at related to a couple of addicts named Matt and Joanne. They were regulars, and Spike had decided he needed to get to know them better. If this couple turned out to be useful, he would find a way to use them to hide his box, maybe at their home, along with clear threats of painful deaths should he be let down.

Firstly, he had to get to know them to see what they were like, and to find out if they could be trusted with such a task. The process of sussing them out might take a while, but there was no time like the present to begin, so Spike picked up his phone and made the call. He would get them over to Bill's gaff right away and treat them to some free gear; they'd be eager to accept such a generous invitation.

Spike made the call and was proved right. The two addicts were only too keen to make the short walk over to Bill's. While waiting, Spike went back to speak with Hathaway.

"Hey, Billy boy, you got any booze in this shithole?" he demanded.

"I got some whisky in the cupboard, and some port left over from Christmas."

"Perfect, that'll do just fine. Sorry, you can't sleep for a while after all, we're having a party. I got guests coming over. Think I'll have some of that whisky now while I'm waiting. Fancy a glass, Billy boy?"

"No thanks, son."

***

Brian Hazell hadn't felt like going back to the bar after his long journey, preferring to go home. He sat at the breakfast bar in his kitchen reading a newspaper, an ashtray to one side, a glass containing a generous measure of his favourite single malt whisky on the other. As he enjoyed a long drag from a cigarette, his phone rang. It was Tommy.

"Tommy, my boy," he answered. "What's happening?"

"It's done, boss."

"Good lad. All go to plan, as usual?"

"Absolutely. The job's a good'un."

"Nice one, Tommy. Go and get yourselves something nice at the club; whatever takes your fancy."

"Cheers, boss."

"Perhaps not Anya, you know, that young Russian bird. I'm saving her for someone."

"No sweat, boss."

Hazell hung up and put the phone down. He folded his paper and started to think things through again, analysing what had happened in Harrogate, along with the trip to Blackburn, before sending young Jamie off to his grave.

Harrogate was the key territory in his mind, and he was determined to do everything and anything to make it a success. He still awaited a response from his earlier text to the potential new informant in Harrogate, but other than that, everything else seemed to have been fixed and reorganised to his satisfaction, as far as Harrogate was concerned.

Spike, who had been brilliant in territories in the past, was new to the area and would surely begin the job of growing business fast. He needed to recruit, get things organised and start selling in volume, while elbowing all competition out of the way. Tommy and Whacko would be on hand to visit to help out whenever anyone needed *persuading* to get out of the way. The ball was in Spike's court now, so he'd better get on with it and succeed.

However, there was a niggle in the back of Hazell's mind. Something bothered him. As he continued to think things through, all the while swigging back his excellent whisky and lighting up one cigarette after another, it became clear what that niggle was. There was still a problem in Harrogate. The same fucking problem that existed two days before.

Louie was still alive.

If Louie recovered, obviously the police were going to question him, and the fact of the matter was the lad knew too much. He should be dead already, but Jamie Bryant

107

had failed to carry out the simple job assigned to him. Hazell cursed him.

"May you rot in hell, Jamie boy," he shouted. "You fucking stupid bastard."

The more Hazell thought about it, the more he knew he had to take action. There was a loose end to tie up. Young Louie couldn't be allowed to recover, it was as simple as that.

The trouble was, Louie was in a hospital with police officers preventing easy access. How was he going to be able to carry this off? Who did he know who would be able to finish the lad off without leaving anything to point in Hazell's direction?

After careful consideration, he decided there was only one candidate he could trust to pull it off: Jonny Beresford.

Brian Hazell picked up his phone and made a call, which was immediately answered.

"Jonny old son, it's Brian. I've got an urgent job for you. Someone needs putting down. All under the radar of course. There's fifty grand in cash in it for you. Interested?"

"Very interested," came Jonny's reply.

"Good. Come and see me at my house, right now. I'll explain what needs doing."

Hazell terminated the call, cutting off Jonny in mid-sentence, and went to fix himself another large whisky. As he took a large swig, his phone pinged. Hazell picked up his phone and read the message in sheer disbelief. He had hit the bullseye!

> **I'm interested. You've caught me at the right time. It'll be a one-off only. How does this work?**

"A one-off?" Hazell laughed. "You stupid bastard! Once you cross that line, I've got you for life."

He composed his reply and sent the message to his new contact.

> **Send me the exact location of young Louie Bryant – I want to send him a get-well card. I need the exact location and the ward number. You do that and you'll have exactly what you need from me. As much and as often as you want it.**

Hazell noticed that the new source had used a different phone number.

"Very clever," he murmured. "But that won't save you from my clutches."

16

Friday

"For fuck's sake!" shouted Brian Hazell as he fumbled over the bedside table searching for his phone.

A text message arriving had woken him from a deep sleep. He found his phone and looked at the screen. It was three twenty-four in the morning.

"Who the fuck is this?" he shouted to no one.

He opened up the message and read it. It was simple, yet beautiful. In just a few words, his new contact had delivered the exact location of the ward where young Louie Bryant was being treated.

Hazell smiled as he recalled his meeting late the previous evening with Jonny Beresford. Jonny was up for it, and all he needed was the location of the target.

Hazell composed a reply explaining that the agreed reward would be delivered in full, as promised. He also explained that all future information received would be likewise rewarded, implying that as a line had been crossed there was now no going back. He suspected he would have to explain that in more detail at some point soon, but that wouldn't be a problem.

He then composed another message to Jonny, giving the details he was waiting for. He hit the send button and replaced his phone on the bedside table.

Time to sleep.

***

Rosie had arrived at Harrogate station early, taking her coffee to the incident room where she was joined by Superintendent Mike Parker. Rosie had known Parker for many years and had an excellent working relationship with him.

The North Yorkshire police force had three sections, Coast, City and County, each of which was managed by a superintendent. Mike Parker was based at Harrogate and was in charge of the county section. He was a tall, dark-haired, graceful man, easy to respect, and carried the aura of authority with him wherever he went. Rosie thought the world of him, but they rarely got the chance to have long and meaningful conversations, like they used to in the good old days. So, she decided to seize the opportunity to talk through what had been happening on their patch during the week.

Parker had heard that George Potter had been involved with a local gang, and was keen to know more about what was happening, as well as learn how Operation Caterpillar was going.

Rosie went through the details, from the incident where a young runner was attacked and nearly murdered, right through to her chat with George Potter the evening before.

"You're bringing George in this morning, are you?" asked Parker.

"Yes, we are. He's coming in with Helen, and we'll be handling that one with great care."

"Absolutely. I suppose this is the last thing Helen needs right now, eh?"

"I know, Mike. It's heartbreaking for the family already, without George getting into trouble. It's lucky that we discovered this was happening before he became more involved. Considering they were prepared to kill another youngster, just because he wanted out, it was just as well that George didn't know anything more about the operation and the players involved."

"Quite right, Rosie. But he's already given a description of the new face in town, hasn't he? What did you say his name was?"

"Spike. We'll get his proper full name in due course, once we've spoken to colleagues over the Pennines. But yes, we have his description so we'll get officers looking out for him. As soon as we have intel, we'll be on him like a rash."

"Do you think Carol may have heard anything about him?"

"I thought of that, and I'll call her as soon as, but I think it's unlikely she'll have heard anything yet. He only arrived yesterday, apparently."

Carol Gosling organised and ran a small local neighbourhood watch type organisation, North Yorkshire Guardians. The NYG gathered information concerning anything that citizens considered suspicious, out of place, or just plain odd. The information was reported to Carol via her website or social media platforms, and she analysed it to see if it should be passed to the police. Carol would then give the information to Rosie, who determined what action, if any, needed to be taken. Rosie first met Carol a few years previously when she was a junior detective, and had developed a close working relationship with her. Over the years, Carol had produced some excellent intel which had helped catch some nasty criminals. One particularly dangerous paedophile had been caught thanks to Carol's intel and was sent to prison for a long time. Carol and her little team continued to produce a great deal of useful intelligence, and NYG was a very useful source.

"What about the lad in hospital then?" asked Parker. "Will he make it?"

"It looks that way. I managed to have a quick chat with him yesterday, but he'd only just woken up so he wasn't able to say much. Besides, his mother, who hadn't seen him for over two months, was there. I'll go back this morning."

"Good. Well done, Rosie. Keep me informed, please."

"Will do. Anyway, Mike, how are you keeping? We must be due a drink sometime soon; how about sometime next week?"

"Sounds like a good plan."

"Does next Tuesday work for you? The Coach and Horses maybe? Or the Fat Badger?"

"The Fat Badger sounds good, but not on Tuesday, Rosie. Tuesdays are my poker nights."

"You play poker? I had no idea."

"Yes, I play at a club in Leeds, whenever I can get away from this place of course."

"So, how much do you lose playing poker?"

"Potentially a lot, Rosie. Thankfully, I've managed to stick to my limits and haven't been tempted to push my luck chasing losses. Some nights though, lady luck's kind to me and I come home smiling."

"Fascinating. We learn something new every day."

"That's just one of the joys of being alive, Rosie," said Parker laughing. "We live and learn. Anyway, I need to get on. I'll catch you later."

"Okay, Mike, I'll keep you up to date with how we're getting on."

"Okay. Thanks, Rosie. Talk soon."

Rosie watched Parker as he exited the room before looking back at her notes. Within a couple of seconds, she heard voices outside the room then the door opened and in walked Chief Inspector Simon Hedley, the area commander responsible for the running of the station.

Rosie always viewed Hedley as an odd character, and could never quite make up her mind whether she liked him or not. Unlike Parker, Hedley did not have an aura of authority about him, and he had nowhere near the same level of respect. The general opinion within the force was that he had brown-nosed his way up the ladder, and Hedley made no secret of the fact that he fully intended to go a lot higher. He had earned the nickname Slimy Simon within the confines of the station, although for obvious reasons it was never mentioned in his presence. The handle was appropriate, and well-suited the greasy Hedley. When Rosie had first shaken his hand a couple of years before, his hand had been clammy causing her to rush off and wash her own hands afterwards. He also had the gait and manner of an obsequious man, like a creepy waiter always seeking to please, especially when more senior officers were around.

But, Rosie knew Hedley to be very capable, so assumed he was, at least to some extent, in his position on merit, so she showed him respect and was ready and willing to cooperate with him at all times.

"Good morning, Rosie," said Hedley as he closed the door behind him.

"Morning, Simon. What's new in Simonland?"

"Simonland?" he asked while sitting down beside Rosie. "Oh yes, I see what you mean. All fine with me, thank you, Rosie. Listen, I was hoping to catch up with you, as I'm concerned about this business with George Potter."

"Yes, quite," said Rosie looking right at Hedley. His hair looked like it hadn't been washed for a while, which didn't help his overall appearance. Directly meeting his light-brown eyes, she asked, "What exactly are you concerned about, Simon?"

"Well, obviously I need to be conscious and aware of Sergeant Potter, well, you know, Helen, at this time. I want to know if she can perform her—"

"Perform her duties?" interrupted Rosie. "If you want my advice, Simon, I'd say that the worst thing we could do is take anything away from Helen at this time. She's going through hell right now with young Jack's illness, and now George is in trouble, she'll be needing all the support we can give her. As long as she's doing her job to her usual high standards, which I understand she is, and until we find out more about what's been happening with George, I suggest we leave things as they are."

115

"Well, yes, I suppose so."

"Can I suggest that we see what George has to say when he arrives here, and take it from there? We could meet to discuss it later."

"Yes, okay, Rosie. That's a good idea."

"I think so. Okay, I need to make a call to my contact at GMP to see what intel he has for me, then I'm off to the hospital to see if Louie, the stabbing victim, is able to talk to me."

"Okay, Rosie, I'll see you later."

"Thanks, Simon."

As Hedley left, Rosie scrolled through her phone contacts looking for DI Jake Singleton at the Greater Manchester Police force.

***

Rosie had met Jake Singleton while on a CID Initial Training course at Wakefield some years before. They had become close friends, along with another trainee from the West Yorkshire force, Scott Hill. Since qualifying and returning to their own patches, they'd remained in touch both professionally and socially to discuss cases, trends in the criminal world, and to share information. They also met for the occasional get-together whenever their busy schedules allowed.

Like Rosie, Jake worked on a team fighting the county lines gangs, so they had a common interest. After Rosie passed on the details of the stabbing incident and the new faces that seemed to have appeared from Lancashire, she was keen to know what, if anything, Jake was able to tell her. She had dialled his number and waited for a response. It came within two rings.

"Yorkshire Rosie," he said. "How lovely to hear from you. What's happening over there? Oh, hang on, it's Yorkshire, so it must be raining," he added jokingly.

"Oh, you are the funny one," Rosie replied. "As it happens, the sun's out this morning. Maybe spring has finally arrived. You'll probably see signs of it over there in a few weeks' time."

"Okay, that's got the pleasantries out of the way." Singleton laughed. "Down to business then; you must be chasing me up on those names you gave me, right?"

"Correct. What have you got?"

"I was going to call you this morning, as I do have news. First of all, Louie Bryant. As you already know, he went missing about nine weeks ago. I'm so glad he's recovering, hopefully he can go home and get on with his life. However, what you might not know, is that we think he was involved with Brian Hazell's mob."

"Brian Hazell? That name rings a bell."

"Yes, it should do. I've mentioned him before during our chats over the last year or so. He's an evil character, local to us, has his fingers in many pies. Money-making businesses, most of which are illegal. But, you know how it is, he's clever and manages to keep out of our reach."

"Oh, I know how they work; lets others get their hands dirty while he gets the profits."

"Yeah, that's about it. And if anyone steps out of line, he has some very large and violent enforcers on the payroll who take care of such problems. We have a long list of missing people, some of whom were most probably dealt with by Hazell's thugs."

"Problem is, let me guess, you can't prove it, right?"

"Exactly. We need hard evidence. Anyway, the word is that Hazell has been expanding his county lines operations farther afield, so the fact that Louie turned up in Harrogate most likely means that Hazell is on your patch."

"Now that is interesting," said Rosie, writing Hazell's name on a notepad. "I wonder if your man Hazell might have been in Harrogate yesterday."

"I wouldn't think so, Hazell is rarely on the front line. He gets others to do all that for him."

"The young lad I spoke to last night said he heard a man's voice talking to the others. The man was clearly in charge, and it wasn't Spike."

"Well, maybe. It's possible, I suppose. If he had something in particular he wanted to do over there, then he might have made the trip. Either way, clearly Hazell has players in Harrogate. We might be working together on this over the next few weeks and months."

"It sounds that way, Jake. So what about the other kid, Aiden Gallagher?"

"Yes, Aiden. Again, we have intel that links him to Hazell's men. He went missing from his home near Blackpool, so we're keen to trace him."

"We heard he was going to Bradford, but that's likely not the case. Apart from that, we know nothing of where he's gone."

"Okay, but it's encouraging that he's been seen alive and well. That's some kind of good news for his family at least."

"What about Freddy and Spike?"

"Yes, they're definitely Hazell's men. Freddy's real name is Adam Fredericks, twenty-five years old, and he's been around a while. However, I've just heard this morning that Freddy was spotted by an officer in Blackburn last night. Maybe he's been moved on by Hazell, in which case young Aiden might be there as well. We're looking into this today."

"Okay. Good luck. What about Spike?"

"Spike is a nasty piece of shit, pardon my French. His name is Sean McKenzie, and he's been all over the place setting up drug selling teams for Hazell. If he's been sent to Harrogate, you've got a real bad boy on your patch. You need to watch him, Rosie. He's an evil young thug who doesn't take prisoners. I'll send a photo and full description over shortly."

"Thanks. We'll get on with looking for him straight away. Anything else, Jake?"

"One more thing. We're looking for another young man who we expected to be with Freddy. His name is Jamie Williams. Does that name ring a bell?"

"Yes, it does. Well, at least Jamie rings a bell. Louie Bryant told me yesterday that the lad who stabbed him was called Jamie."

"That's interesting… and frightening at the same time. It could mean that Jamie was told to kill Louie, but failed. Hazell doesn't take kindly to failure, Rosie, which means Jamie could be in danger himself. We need to find him as soon as possible."

"If it's not already too late."

"Yes, quite."

"Okay, Jake, I've got to go to the hospital now and see if I can question Louie. Thanks for the update, particularly the name Brian Hazell."

"I have a feeling you'll hear a lot more about Brian Hazell, unfortunately."

"I'd love to help you bring him down, Jake."

"That sounds like a great plan."

"Okay. Thanks again, Jake. Talk soon."

Rosie hung up, grabbed her things, and headed to the door.

17

A man in his early forties, wearing a white lab coat, walked across the Knaresborough Road in Harrogate. He turned into Lancaster Park Road and walked the short distance to the main gates of Harrogate hospital. It was a pleasant day, but spring had not yet arrived. It was still unseasonally cold.

His blond curly hair had been cut and dyed dark brown, and his thick moustache had been shaved off. He arrived at the gate and turned into the hospital grounds before walking into the main entrance. He knew exactly where to go, and headed off to his destination.

As he paced purposefully down the main corridor a nurse was walking towards him heading for the main reception.

"Good morning," said the man as they passed.

"Good morning, Doctor," replied the nurse.

The man smiled and continued on his way.

***

Rosie parked her car in the car park at Harrogate hospital and walked towards the main entrance with a viciously cold wind blowing into her face.

An elderly gentleman, who was also making his way to the hospital entrance, had one hand on his walking stick while the other clutched the lapels of his jacket in an effort to keep the chill away from his chest.

"Can I help you, sir?" she said as she slipped her hand inside his arm. "Let me walk you to the foyer."

"Thank you very much," he said. "Should've worn more layers today."

Rosie helped the man to the reception desk, said her goodbyes and left. She headed down the corridor on her way to see Louie Bryant.

***

Spike stood at the door of a flat on the Jennyfield housing estate, a mile and a half or so from the centre of Harrogate. It had taken him just a few minutes to drive from Bill Hathaway's home. In his hand was his rusty old metal box.

He'd already knocked on the door a couple of times, but so far had no response. He tried again, banging his fist on the opaque reinforced glass. This time it worked, and the door opened to reveal a sickly-looking young man, Matt Hague, peering through the gap at the frightening sight of Spike staring back at him.

"What d'ya want?" said Hague. "Oh, it's you."

"Yeah, it's me," said Spike. "You look like shit this morning."

"Er, yeah. Still wasted on that shit you gave us last night."

"I've come to see you, Matt. Are you fucking letting me in or do I have to barge through?"

Matt slowly opened the door to allow Spike to enter.

122

"Fuck me," said Spike moving through to what passed as a lounge. "It's a shithole in here, Matt. Don't your missus ever clean this gaff?"

Matt didn't respond. He was having trouble waking up.

"Where is your missus?" Spike demanded.

"Who? Oh, you mean Jo. She's asleep. She won't be waking up for a while."

"Okay, that's good cos I want to talk with you. Like I said last night, I've taken over round here."

"Yeah, right. Okay. Tell me again, what happened to Freddy?"

"Freddy's been moved on. I'm in charge now, so you get all your gear from me."

"Yeah, cool. Whatever."

"Good. So, I want you to work with me for a while, to help me recruit a team. I might even move in here with you sometime soon, although looking at the state of the place, I might not. But I'll be here a lot. In return, I'll help you with cheaper shit. In fact, some of it'll be free, if you play your cards right."

"Free?" said Matt, getting more interested in proceedings.

"Yeah, free. Sometimes, that is. Not all the time. You look after me, I'll look after you."

"Okay."

"Yeah, cos I need you to do something for me, like really soon." Spike held up the metal box he was carrying. "See this box?"

"Yeah, I see it."

"I want you to find a hiding place for it, to keep it safe. Somewhere no one knows about. A safe place where no one, and I mean no one, can find it. Can you do that for me?"

"Yeah, I suppose."

"No supposing, Matt. That ain't good enough. I need somewhere a hundred percent safe."

"You can keep it here if you like," said Matt while sweeping his arm around.

"What, here in this flat? Are you fucking kidding me? I need somewhere else. Totally secure."

"I don't know anywhere else."

"Well think about it, Matt. And when you've thought about it, come and see me at Bill's flat. You know where I mean, don't you? You were there last night."

"Yeah, I remember. And I know Bill, he's an old mate of my dad's. They both have an allotment up over—"

"I don't give a shit about fucking allotments, Matt. Just find me a safe place and come and see me when you have."

"Yeah, will do."

"And when you do, I'll give you some freebies, Matty boy. You get my drift?"

"I do, Spike."

"But here's the downside," said Spike, his eyes drilling into Matt's. "You ever lose my box, or try to open it, or tell anyone about my box, I *will* kill you."

There was a pause as Spike let that statement sink in.

"Do you understand what I just told you?"

"Yeah, yeah. I understand."

Without losing eye contact, Spike withdrew a large knife from his side pocket, lifted it and gently rested its tip against the flesh at the top of Hague's neck, just above the thyroid cartilage, his Adam's apple.

"And do you think I can kill you, if I want to?" continued Spike.

Hague's eyes were wide open, his mouth gaping wide, in shock as he felt the sharp tip of the blade threatening to pierce the skin. His natural urge was to swallow, to gulp due to his total fear, but knew that if he did his Adam's apple would push against the sharp blade. He hardly dared to breath as he looked at the thug in front of him. He was under no illusions as to the evils that Spike was capable of.

"Yes," Hague whispered, careful not to accidentally jerk forward. "I think you can."

"Can what?"

"Kill me."

"Yeah, too fucking right I can. And do you believe that I'll kill you if you fuck up?"

"Yeah. I believe you. Please put the blade away."

"Yeah, good, Matty boy," said Spike as he withdrew the knife and slipped it back in his pocket. "You just do me proud, and I'll look after you and, what's her name?"

"Jo. Joanne."

"Joanne, yeah. Don't say nothing to her, mind. But I'll look after you both if you do what I ask. Meanwhile, here's something to keep you going."

Spike threw a pack at the addict. Matt's eyes lit up at the prosect of getting more free gear, and he tried to catch it. He was too slow, and watched as it dropped onto the floor. He bent down to pick it up, but as he stood Spike moved closer. There was no more than three inches between their faces.

"You and me are gonna be a great team, Matty boy. You do what I ask, you'll be looked after."

"Okay, Spike."

"Good lad."

Spike grabbed his box, turned and made his way out of the flat. He threw the box in the stolen car, jumped in and made his way back to Bill Hathaway's flat.

***

The man wearing the doctor's lab coat looked at his watch. It was time. He felt inside his coat pocket, carefully pulled out a syringe, and examined it. There was nothing but fresh air inside. He replaced it and walked purposefully towards a room in the Intensive Care Unit.

The policeman outside the room looked at him as he approached.

"Top of the morning," said the man, in his very best Irish accent.

"Good morning," replied the officer. "I haven't seen you—"

"How's the wee young lad this morning?" interrupted the man as he passed by, opened the door and looked in. "Ah, he's doing just fine, so he is. Thank you, officer."

The man entered and closed the door behind him. He looked at the sleeping boy, then turned to examine the intravenous infusion set-up. It wasn't what he'd wanted to see as tampering with it would be difficult. He couldn't risk leaving any evidence of what he was about to do, so would have to consider another method. Next, he carefully pulled back the sheets covering the patient and noticed the dressing covering the wound at the top of his leg.

"Oh, that's ideal," mumbled the man as he carefully peeled the dressing away, revealing the fresh stab wound. "Just perfect."

He then found the notes on the end of the bed and scanned them to see that the lad was still on painkillers, and guessed that he would be out for the count for a while. Just in case, he had placed a plastic bag containing a rag doused with chloroform in another coat pocket, along with other bits and pieces that might be useful. And, as a last resort, a loaded pistol was tucked away in a holster, should he have to shoot his way out of trouble.

But that shouldn't be necessary, he thought as he dipped his hand into a pocket and found a spray he had brought to numb the flesh around the wound. He applied a few blasts of the cold substance before finding the syringe and carefully pushing it into the wound on the young lad's groin. The chances of the needle's entry into the flesh being detected afterwards would be substantially less likely.

The man's military training meant that finding the inferior vena cava, was an easy task. He injected the contents of the syringe into the vein and directly into the young man's bloodstream.

Louie Bryant had remained sleeping throughout the process, and within little more than sixty seconds the man had exited the room, passing the police officer on his way out.

"The lad's doing just fine," he said as he walked away. "No doubt I'll be seeing you later, officer."

***

Rosie walked along the corridor towards the ward in ICU where Louie was recovering. As she approached a corner a few yards from the ward and was about to turn, a man came around and they nearly collided.

"Oh my," said Rosie looking at the man in his white lab coat. "Sorry, Doctor. That was a close one."

"No problem at all," said the man in a broad Irish accent as he passed on by. "Think nothing of it. Good day to you."

"Good day to you, Doctor," said Rosie as she watched him walk away.

She turned and looked at the officer sitting outside the ward.

"Good morning," said Rosie.

"Good morning, ma'am."

"Everything okay?"

"Everything's fine. Doctor's just been in and said the lad's doing well."

"Good."

Rosie entered the room and saw that Louie was sleeping. She glanced at the tubes and wires leading up to the monitors and other machines. None of it meant anything to her, but the screen showing Louie's pulse indicated that he was steady, even though his breathing seemed to be a little heavy and laboured. She watched him for a while before going back outside.

"I was hoping to question him this morning, but I'll have to wait till he wakes up. I'll go and get a coffee and come back later."

"Yes, ma'am."

At that moment, an alarm went off inside the room. Rosie rushed in to see that the monitor showing his pulse was flatlining.

"Oh my god," she shrieked.

Two nurses rushed down the corridor, pushing past Rosie to get to young Louie's bedside.

"You need to leave now," said one of the nurses to Rosie.

"Okay," said Rosie as she left the room and closed the door.

A doctor rushed down the corridor and barged through into the side ward. Rosie stood outside in shock as she listened to the noises from the room.

As the medical team were doing their best to bring Louie back round, Rosie looked up the corridor and groaned. Louie's mother, Camilla, was coming towards her with a warm smile on her face.

"Hello," she chirped. "How's Louie doing this morning?"

18

Rosie knew exactly where the chapel at the hospital was situated, and had taken the distraught Camilla Bryant there after the shocking events in her son's ICU ward.

There was nothing more the medical team could do. Louie Bryant had died of heart failure. It was too early to know what had led to his death, and the best the doctor could guess at that early stage was heart failure caused by an air embolism.

A post mortem would hopefully reveal more, but for the time being all Rosie knew was that Louie, who had been recovering nicely from his ordeal, was dead. She was getting a nasty feeling about what had happened, and beginning to wonder if something sinister had taken place, right under her nose. On the way to the chapel with Camilla she had seen the doctor once again, the Irishman she'd almost bumped into in the corridor. She'd have liked to have asked him how Louie was when he saw him.

But she had to focus on Camilla, who was now the priority. She would search for that doctor some other time. Poor Camilla, after losing her son a couple of months before, had found him and he'd wanted to come home, when suddenly and tragically, he had slipped away from her once again, this time forever. It was all too much.

Rosie's arms were wrapped around Camilla, holding her tight as she wept bitterly, sinking her head as far as she could into Rosie's shoulder. Rosie said nothing for several minutes until Camilla ran out of tears. Eventually she managed to say something.

"Why? Just why did this happen?"

"I don't know, sweetheart," said Rosie. She had suspicions that something sinister had happened, but wasn't going to share those thoughts with Camilla. "The doctor said it may have been air in Louie's bloodstream that reached his heart, but we don't know yet. We'll try our best to find out."

"But he was fine last night, Rosie. What happened?"

"We don't know yet, Camilla. Louie had surgery on Wednesday evening, and was on a drip, so it's possible that air had entered his bloodstream at some point and wasn't detected. Once it reached his heart, it was too late. I'm so sorry, the doctors did their best, but sadly it wasn't enough."

Camilla started crying again.

"But know this, Camilla," Rosie continued. "This is now murder, and I, along with my team will do everything we can to catch the people responsible for Louie's death and bring them to justice. I want justice for Louie, and justice for you."

"Thank you, Rosie," sobbed Camilla.

"I've asked for a family liaison officer to come and see you. You'll get all the help you need, and if you want to ask me anything at all, just call me."

Brain Hazell had been sitting at his fancy breakfast bar reading his paper, drinking coffee and chain-smoking, while waiting for news from Harrogate. If everything goes to plan, he thought, there'll be nothing to stop me from having a monopoly on the drugs business in that quaint little town.

He laughed as he picked up his cigarette and took a long satisfying drag. As he exhaled and watched the circles of smoke he had expertly created, his phone buzzed. It was the news he had been waiting for. He rested his cigarette on the ashtray and picked up his phone to read the message.

> **Mission accomplished. The lad's gone. Waited back till I got confirmation he didn't make it. Leaving Harrogate now.**

"Outstanding!" shouted Hazell. He composed a text and sent it.

> **Good work. See you shortly when you collect your cash.**

"Now, that's what I call a result. Two useless little bastards dealt with and on their way to the next life, a new and better team leader in Harrogate, all loose ends tied up, and as a bonus I've got myself a new informant. Not a bad week's work."

He reached for a fresh cigarette and lit it up, inhaled deeply and produced another couple of perfect smoke rings. He had a big grin on his face.

"Brian Hazell, you're a fucking genius."

***

Rosie had returned to the incident room at Harrogate police station where she found Masoud, French and Leblanc. The atmosphere was flat after the news of Louie Bryant's death, and Rosie was still visibly shaken by what had happened.

"I've got a nasty feeling something happened this morning at the hospital," she said. "I'm finding it hard to accept that Louie's death was just an unlucky setback in his treatment and recovery."

"You think someone got to him, boss?" asked French.

"I don't know, but I'm suspicious, John."

"The post mortem might reveal something," added Masoud.

"Maybe, maybe not, Faz. What I do know is that a doctor, a man with a strong Irish accent, whom PC Milligan had never seen before, entered the ward a short while before I got there. He was inside for a minute or so, before leaving and nearly bumping into me when I arrived. I didn't see his name, but when I spoke to the hospital's HR manager, I was told that the only Irish doctor currently working there is a Doctor Kayleigh Sullivan. Well, I saw Dr Sullivan and can confirm that she is very much a she, and was not the doctor that PC Milligan and I saw. I smell a rat."

"Why did PC Milligan allow this unknown doctor in the ward?" asked Leblanc.

"Good question, Max. Milligan is young and was perhaps hoodwinked into assuming this man was allowed inside. He will be hauled in and grilled about it, but that's not our concern. What we need to do, apart from waiting for the post mortem report, is to find out how the bloody hell this man knew how to find the ward where Louie was being treated."

"Good point," said French. "It was supposed to be a closely guarded secret."

"Precisely! I don't believe this individual wandered around the whole hospital looking for a ward with a copper outside. I reckon someone must have told him."

"Who?" asked Leblanc.

"I haven't got a clue," answered Rosie. "That's what we've got to find out. I'm going to have a word with a friend in PSD to see how I should approach this."

There was a silence in the room as that thought sank in. Bent coppers were dangerous and for obvious reasons were not popular with the majority of good, hard-working police officers in any force. The Professional Standards Department (PSD) handled misconduct and complaints against police officers and staff. If there really was a rogue officer passing information onto criminals for personal gain, whether it be for money or anything else, the PSD would look into it, but they would need more than Rosie's gut feeling to investigate. They would need evidence, which Rosie would do her best to obtain.

"Listen, guys," Rosie continued. "We're all fighting county lines crimes, of which there are plenty. And we've just learned of a new player in town, Sean McKenzie, known as Spike. We've got to get on with watching him. And we also know that Spike works for a certain OCG boss called Brian Hazell, a character we're learning a great deal about. He's not a nice person. In fact he's a downright nasty piece of work. Now, here's the thing, if Hazell has got one of our colleagues in his pocket, we've got our work cut out. I want us all to keep this in mind at all times, and everything you hear concerning a potential leak, everything you discover, no matter how trivial it may appear, you run by me so we can get the clearest picture possible. We're going to fight Hazell and his merry men with all our might, and if there is a bent cop here, we're going to help the PSD bring them down. That clear?"

"Yes, boss," replied a chorus of voices.

***

Still at the breakfast bar, with a fresh mug of coffee sitting alongside an overflowing ashtray, Brian Hazell was making progress reading his newspaper. He had just finished the sports pages when his phone buzzed once again. He picked it up and read the message.

> **WTF? The kid's dead! You had him murdered? If you'd told me, I would never have helped you!**

Hazell laughed as he composed a reply.

> **Hard fucking luck. Your job is to give me what I ask for, my job is to do what I want with it. You've got**

your reward, enjoy it – when I want something else from you I'll be in touch.

Within a minute, Hazell's phone buzzed again with a reply.

You must be joking! I'm not doing this anymore. You've got what you wanted, that's the end of this arrangement.

Hazell quickly composed his answer to that statement.

I NEVER JOKE. And you WILL do this again. Remember, you're in my pocket now. You crossed the line, there's no going back! And don't ever forget, you're an accomplice now. If you even think about not complying I'll drop you right in the SHIT!

Hazell waited a few minutes before replacing his phone on the breakfast bar. He knew his new contact would get the message, and he would be in touch whenever he needed something.

***

Rosie sat alone in her office, mulling over the events of the last few days. The recent county lines scenario had been eventful, not only with the murder of Louie Bryant, but the arrival of a new player in Harrogate, a nasty character known as Spike. Also, there was a new OCG boss to think about, Brian Hazell. Although not on her patch, she would do her best to be involved in his investigation by keeping in regular contact with DI Jake Singleton from GMP.

Her thoughts were interrupted by a knock on her door.

"Come in," she shouted. The door opened and Fazli Masoud entered Rosie's office. "Faz, just the person I wanted to see, sit down. What can I do for you?"

"I've been thinking about what you said, you know, about a leak here at the station. Do you really think someone here gave away the details of that ward where Louie was being treated?"

"That's what I wanted to talk over with you, Faz. I want to see if what I'm thinking makes sense, or if I'm going bonkers. To put the question regarding Louie another way, was he murdered on Wednesday evening, or this morning at Harrogate hospital?"

"That's a hell of a question, boss. Louie might have died due to an issue caused while in surgery, or during the recovery process."

"What's known as perioperative death, yes. In which case, he was murdered on Wednesday. But who was that doctor I saw today? With the Irish accent? Who no one at the hospital seems to actually know, and happened to be in Louie's ward moments before he died?

"I don't know boss, good question. What did your contact in PSD say?"

"No evidence, so the advice is to leave it alone, at least until after the post mortem. If it becomes clear there's foul play involved, then we may have the start of a case. Until then, I mustn't bother them with nothing more than rumours or my gut feelings."

"I see. So, what do we do now?"

"Well, I don't know about you Faz, but I'm going to get on with my job, to the best of my ability, just like I always do. But I will be keeping a bloody good lookout for anything suspicious, odd, peculiar, or anything that might back up my suspicion that Brian Hazell has an informant here at this station."

"Count me in, boss. I hate bent coppers, and if there's one here, I'll do anything I can to bring them to justice."

"Then let's do just that, Faz. We get on with our jobs, we start watching Spike, we fight all county lines in and around Harrogate and bring as many criminals as we can to justice. But, if there is a leak at this station, you and I will stay on the lookout for any clues as to their identity, and we'll discuss what to do about nailing them. It'll be our secret mission. Agreed?"

"Agreed."

"I held Camilla in my arms this morning, while she sobbed her heart out. Just when she'd been reunited with her missing son, full of hope for a new start with him, he was snatched away. I think he was murdered this morning, and over time I intend to prove it. And let's face it, if Brian Hazell has got an informant here, he's going to be getting information and favours that we'll soon notice, Faz."

"Absolutely."

"Good," said Rosie before looking towards her office window. She paused for a few seconds, thinking. She then thumped her fist down on her desk, causing an empty coffee cup, and Masoud, to jump. "Any bastard here who thinks they can get away with betraying the trust of colleagues, as well as the public, and participate in the murder of a young lad, and god knows what else, has got another thing coming. Right, Faz?"

"Right, boss."

"Okay. Come on, let's get back to the incident room. We need to start watching Spike. I want him off the streets of Harrogate asap."

***

Matt Hague found himself staring at one of the objects hanging on the wall in Bill Hathaway's hallway. It wasn't the old, faded photographs of loved ones that Bill had hung up over the years that had caught his attention, nor was it the cheap print of a Turner masterpiece that was suspended at an awkward angle, holding a generous collection of dust on the top of the frame. What Hague was looking at was a collection of keys hanging from hooks fixed to an old wooden keyholder.

"You've got a lot of keys up there, Bill," he said to the old man.

"You what, son?"

"You've got a lot of keys on those hooks. You've only got one door here, and you haven't got a car. What are the rest of them for?"

"Most of them are old keys I haven't chucked away. I only need two these days, the front door and the key to the shed at my allotment."

"Oh, yeah. My dad's got an allotment near yours. I remember seeing you there years ago. When do you go there?"

"I don't, son. Haven't been for ages. I'm too old and poorly."

"Yeah, I see what you mean."

Hague kept looking at the keys while thinking. An idea was forming in his mind.

"Which key's the one for the shed then, Bill?"

"The one on the far left."

"Oh, right. Listen, I gotta go and see Spike."

Hague got up and went to the bedroom where Spike was just finishing a phone call.

"What the fuck do you want, Matty boy?"

"I've just had a brilliant idea, Spike."

"Oh yeah? Well, it had better be good, or I'm not interested. Just had some bad news."

"What news?"

"Tommy and Whacko are coming over, they'll be here in twenty minutes. They're a couple of evil bastards, Matty boy, so I suggest you fuck off, right now."

"Oh, right. I'll be on my way, then."

"Before you go, I need your help with a problem. I gotta hide that fucking box of mine before they get here. Take it back to your gaff, will you? Just till they've gone."

"I can do better than that, Spike. That's my brilliant idea. I know exactly where to hide that box. Somewhere no one's ever going to find it, and I can do it right now."

"Oh yeah? Where's this place, that's so fucking good, no one's ever going to find it?"

"I'll bury it at Bill's allotment. It's perfect. I've been there before, so I know exactly where to hide it. It'll be safe there."

"I don't like it. What if someone sees you and helps themselves after you've gone?"

"They won't, I'll make sure no one sees me. And your mates, what's their names, Tommy and Whacko, will never find that box where I'm hiding it."

"You just listen to me, Matty boy," Spike said as he walked over and stood right in front of Hague, staring into his eyes. He pulled his knife out once again and rested the blade against his left cheek. "If anything happens that stops me from getting that box back, anything at all, I will kill you. You know that, don't you?"

"Yeah, I know that, Spike," Hague answered, once again willing himself not to move. He actually stopped breathing as Spike moved the blade over and rested it against his right cheek.

"Well, I'm not sure you're getting the message, Matty boy," hissed Spike as he moved the knife down and pushed the tip against the underside of his mandible. He pushed the blade just enough to make a small cut into the skin. "If I'm gonna trust you with that box, I need to know you're gonna guard it with your life. Will you do that for me?"

"Y-yes, Spike," stuttered Hague, taking great care as he spoke. Each movement of his jaw risked the blade going deeper into his flesh. "You already told me you'd kill me if I fuck up. But you did say if I look after you, you'll look after me too, yeah?"

"I did say that, Matty boy. So, my box is a hundred percent safe in your hands, yeah?"

"Yes, Spike. Honestly, that place is perfect, and I can do it right now. Give me the box, I'll get it done, so you

141

can give me more of that great shit for me and Jo. How about that?"

"Okay," said Spike thinking about this suggestion. "And you know that whenever I ask for it back, which I will, you'll hand it over to me, yeah?"

"Absolutely. Within an hour."

"And you'll never open it?"

"Wouldn't dream of it. It's locked anyway, innit. Come on, Spike, put that blade away and hand the box over. Let's get it done, yeah? Before your mates turn up."

Spike replaced the knife in his pocket, turned round and reached behind a cupboard. He picked up his metal box and held it out. Hague went to grab it, but Spike didn't release it for a few seconds. He was nervous about handing it over for obvious reasons, but the risk of giving it to a smackhead to look after was definitely the lesser of two evils compared to the unthinkable possibility of having it discovered by Tommy and Whacko, who were only moments away. He had no choice, so released his grip on the box, allowing Hague to take it away.

Hague left the room, stopped in the hallway and grabbed the key to Bill's shed. Before moving towards the front door, he took a few deep breaths to recompose himself. He rubbed his hand under his chin and looked down, there was blood on his fingers which he wiped on his old, dirty jeans. He then dabbed the sleeve of his hoodie under his chin in an effort to wipe away any remaining blood, before opening the door and leaving Bill Hathaway's flat.

While striding towards Hathaway's allotment, the metal box tucked under his arm, his thoughts turned towards

142

exactly where he would hide it. He knew the ideal spot, and he smiled as he thought about how perfect it was, a place no one would ever think of looking. And of course, the beautiful thing was that surely, all the while only he knew the exact whereabouts of that box, Spike would never dream of harming him.

Things were looking up for Matt Hague and Joanne Chapman.

About the Author

Phil Holmes was born in Hampshire, England, and 'emigrated' to the northern spa town Harrogate in the county of North Yorkshire where he has lived for many years. Since school, he has worked as a painter and decorator, a double glazing salesman and MD of a manufacturing company, to mention just a few. He then went on to run his own office supplies business which he sold in late 2019.

These days Phil, who is addicted to golf, spends as much time as he dares on the golf course, works in the accountancy and bookkeeping business he owns with his wife, watches lots of sport, all the while working on writing novels.

Phil's loves include music, playing golf and watching sport. His dislikes include injustice, bad weather (especially on golf days) and has a life-long hatred of cheese!

A few years ago he began to work on an idea for a series of stories featuring a police detective named DCI Rosie Marks, who leads a team of officers fighting County Lines and related crimes in North Yorkshire under the project name 'Operation Caterpillar'.

The Rosie Marks series is being launched from 2025, beginning with an introductory novella named 'County Lines'.

Phil lives in Harrogate with his wife. He has three children and four grandchildren.

www.philsholmes.com

Printed in Great Britain
by Amazon